THE VALKYRIES

Also by Paulo Coelho

✺

The Alchemist
The Pilgrimage

THE VALKYRIES

An Encounter with Angels

Paulo Coelho

Translated by Alan R. Clarke

HarperCollins *Publishers* India

HarperCollins *Publishers* India

HarperCollins*Publishers*
1 London Bridge Street,
London, SE1 9GF, United Kingdom

First published in Portuguese as *As Valkirias* by
Editoria Rocca Ltd. Brazil 1992
English Translation prepared by Alan R. Clarke
English Translation published by
HarperCollins *Publishers* USA 1995

Published in 1996 by Thorsons

31th impression 2019

ISBN 13: 978 81 7223 540 6

FICTION / PHILOSOPHY

HarperCollins *Publishers*
A-75, Sector 57, NOIDA, Uttar Pradesh – 201301, India
1 London Bridge Street, London, SE1 9GF, United Kingdom
2 Bloor Street East, Toronto, Ontario M4W 1A8, Canada
Lvl 13, 201 Elizabeth Street (PO Box A565, NSW, 1235),
Sydney NSW 2000, Australia
195 Broadway, New York, NY 10007, USA

Printed and bound at
Thomson Press (India) Ltd.

And an angel descended
where they were
and the glory of the Lord
shone all about them.

Luke 2:9

THE VALKYRIES

THE VALKYRIE

PROLOGUE

"Something that is of great importance to me?" J. thought for a few moments before responding. "Magic."

"No, something else," Paulo insisted.

"Women," J. said. "Magic and women."

Paulo laughed.

"They're important to me, too," he said. "Although marriage has slowed me down a bit."

It was J.'s turn to laugh.

"A bit," he said. "Just a bit."

Paulo filled his master's glass with wine. It had been four months since they had seen each other, and this was a quite special night. Paulo wanted to talk for a while longer, build the suspense, before giving J. the package he had brought.

"I used to imagine the great masters as people who were far removed from the world," he said to J. "If you had answered me that way a few years ago, I think I would have abandoned my apprenticeship."

"You should have done that," J. said, sipping at his wine. "And I would have found a beautiful woman disciple to take your place."

They drank the entire bottle of wine as they sat talking in the restaurant located on the top floor of J.'s hotel. They spoke of work, magic, and women. J. was euphoric about the huge contract he had just negotiated for the Dutch multinational for which he worked. And Paulo was excited about the package he had brought with him.

"Let's have another bottle," Paulo said.

"In honor of what?"

"Your coming to Rio de Janeiro. . . . The beautiful view from the window over there. . . . And the present I've brought you."

J. looked out the window to see Copacabana beach sparkling below. "The view deserves a toast," he said, signaling to the waiter.

When they were halfway through the second bottle, Paulo placed the package on the table.

Looking at J., he said, "If you were to ask me what is important to me, I would say: my master. It was he who taught me to understand that love is the only thing that never fails. He who had the patience to lead me along the intricate paths of magic. He who had the courage and dignity, despite his powers, to present himself always as a person with some doubts and with certain weaknesses. He who helped me to understand the forces that can transform our lives."

"We've had a lot of wine," J. said. "I don't want to get serious."

"I'm not talking about serious things. I'm talking about joyful things. I'm talking about love."

He pushed the package to J.'s side of the table. "Open it."

"What is this?"

"A way of saying thank you. And of passing on to others all the love you taught me."

J. opened the package. It contained almost two hundred typed pages, on the first of which was written *"The Alchemist."*

Paulo's eyes were gleaming.

"It's a new book," he said. "Look at the next page."

There was an inscription written in longhand: "For J., the alchemist who knows and uses the secrets of the Great Work."

Paulo had anxiously awaited this moment. He had been able to keep completely secret the fact that he was writing a new book, even though he knew that J. had really liked his previous book.

"This is the original manuscript," Paulo continued. "I'd like you to read it before I send it to the publisher."

He tried to read the expression in his master's eyes, but they were impenetrable.

"I have meetings all day tomorrow," J. said, "so I'll be able to read it only at night. Let's have lunch two days from now."

Paulo had been expecting a different reaction. He thought that J. would be happy, and moved by the inscription.

"Let's do that," said Paulo, hiding his disappointment. "I'll be back in two days."

J. called for the check. They walked silently to the elevator. J. pushed the button for the eleventh floor.

When the elevator stopped at his floor, J. pushed the Emergency button to hold the door open. Then he approached Paulo and said, "May the Lamb of God protect you," making a sign on the forehead of his disciple.

Paulo embraced his master and said good night. Resetting the button, J. stepped out of the elevator.

"Why didn't you make copies of the original?" he asked, as the door began to close.

"In order to give God the chance to make it disappear, if that was his will."

"Wise decision," Paulo heard J. say as the door closed. "I hope that the literary critics never discover where it is."

✺

They met two days later, at the same restaurant.

J. began, "There are certain secrets of alchemy described in your book. Secrets I never discussed with you. And you presented them quite correctly."

Paulo was delighted. This was just what he wanted to hear.

"Well, I've been studying," he explained.

"No, you haven't been studying," J. said. "Yet what you've written about is correct."

"I can't fool him," Paulo thought. "I'd like him to think I'm dedicated, but I can't fool him."

He looked outside. The sun was glaring, and the beach was crowded.

"What do you see in that immense sky?" J. asked.

"Clouds."

"No," J. said. "You see the soul of the rivers. Rivers that have just been reborn in the sea. They will rise to the sky, and remain there until, for whatever reason, they once again become rain and fall to earth.

"The rivers return to the mountains, but carry with them the wisdom of the sea."

J. poured himself some mineral water. He didn't usually drink during the day.

"That is how you discovered those secrets we had never discussed," J. said. "You are a river. You have already run down to the sea, and you know its wisdom. You have died and been reborn many times. All you have to do is remember."

Paulo was happy. It was a kind of praise: His master said that he had "discovered secrets." But he was unable to ask openly which secrets they were.

"I have a new task for you," J. said. Silently, he thought, *It has to do with your book. Because I know it's very important to you, and it doesn't deserve to be destroyed.* But Paulo didn't need to hear about that.

❀

One week later, J. and Paulo walked together through the airport. Paulo wanted to know more about the task that his master had assigned him the week before, but J. carefully avoided conversation. They sat down at a table in the cafeteria.

"We were able to have dinner together only twice during my stay here in Rio," J. began, "and this is our third. It's in observance of the saying 'Anything that occurs once can never occur again. But, should it happen twice, it will surely happen a third time.'"

J. was trying to avoid the subject, but Paulo persevered. He knew now that his master had liked the book's dedication, because he had overheard a conversation between J. and the receptionist at the hotel. And later, one of J.'s friends had referred to Paulo as "the book's author."

He must have told a number of people about it—there was, after all, only one copy of the original. *Vanity of vanities,* he said to himself. He thanked God for having given him a master so human.

"I want to ask you about the task," Paulo said once again. "I don't want to ask 'how' or 'where,' because I know you won't tell me."

"Well, that's one thing you've learned in all this time," J. laughed.

"In one of our conversations," Paulo continued, "you told me about a man named Gene, who was able to do what you are now asking of me. I'm going to look for him."

"Did I give you his address?"

7

"You mentioned that he lived in the United States, in the California desert. It shouldn't be too hard to get there."

"No, it isn't."

As they spoke, Paulo became aware that the voice on the public address system was continually announcing flight departures. He began to feel tense, fearing there wouldn't be enough time to complete their conversation.

"Even though I don't want to know 'how' or 'where,' you taught me that there is a question we should always ask as we undertake something. I'm asking you that question now: Why? Why must I do this?"

"Because people always kill the things they love," J. replied.

As Paulo pondered the mystery of this answer, once again he heard a departure announced.

"That's my plane," J. said. "I have to go."

"But I don't understand your answer to my question."

Asking Paulo to pay the bill, J. quickly wrote something on a paper napkin.

Placing the napkin on the table in front of his disciple, J. said, "During the last century, a man wrote about what I've just said to you. But it's been true for many generations."

Paulo picked up the napkin. For a fraction of a second, he thought it might contain a magic formula. But it was a verse from a poem.

And each man kills the thing he loves,
By all let this be heard,
Some do it with a bitter look,
Some with a flattering word,
The coward does it with a kiss,
The brave man with a sword.

The waiter came with the change, but Paulo didn't notice. He couldn't stop looking at those terrible words.

"And so, the task," J. said after a long silence. "It's needed to break that curse."

"One way or another," Paulo said slowly, "I have wound up destroying what I've loved. I've seen my dreams fall apart just when I seemed about to achieve them. I always thought that was just the way life was. My life and everyone else's."

"The curse can be broken," J. repeated, "if you complete the task."

They walked through the noisy airport in silence. J. was thinking about the books that his disciple had written. He thought about Chris, Paulo's wife. He knew that Paulo was being drawn toward the magical initiation that appears at one time or another in everyone's life.

He knew that Paulo was on the brink of seeing one of his greatest dreams realized.

And this meant danger, because J.'s disciple was like all human beings: He was going to find that he did not necessarily deserve all that he had received.

But he didn't tell Paulo any of this.

"The women of your country are beautiful," J. said with a smile, as they arrived at the passport control line. "I hope I can come back."

But Paulo spoke seriously.

"So that's what the task is for," he said, as his master handed over his passport for stamping. "To break the curse."

And J. answered, just as seriously. "It's for love. For victory. And for the glory of God."

THEY HAD BEEN DRIVING FOR almost six hours. For the hundredth time, he asked the woman at his side if they were on the right road.

For the hundredth time, she looked at the map. Yes, they were going the right way, even though their surroundings were green, and a river ran nearby, and there were trees along the road.

"I think we should stop at a gas station and check," she said.

They drove on without speaking, listening to old songs on the radio. Chris knew that it wasn't necessary to stop at a gas station, because they were on the right road—even if the scenery around them was completely different from what they had expected. But she knew her husband well. Paulo was nervous and uncertain, thinking that she was misreading the map. He would feel better if they stopped and asked.

"What are we doing here?"

"I have a task to perform," he answered.

"Strange task," she said.

Very strange, he thought. *To speak to his guardian angel.*

"Okay," she said after a while, "you're here to speak to your guardian angel. Meanwhile, how about talking a bit with me?"

But he said nothing, concentrating on the road, thinking again that she had made a mistake about the route. *No point in insisting,* she thought. She was hoping they would come upon a gas station soon.

They had headed out on their journey straight from Los Angeles International Airport. She was afraid that Paulo was tired, and might fall asleep at the wheel. They didn't seem to be anywhere near their destination.

I should have married an engineer, she said to herself.

She had never gotten used to his life—taking off suddenly, looking for sacred pathways, swords, conversing with angels, doing everything possible to move further along the path to magic.

He has always wanted to leave everything behind.

❁

She remembered their first date. They had slept together, and within a week she had moved her art work table into his apartment. Their friends said that Paulo was a sorcerer, and one night Chris had telephoned the minister of the Protestant church she attended, asking him to say a prayer for her.

But during that first year, he had said not one word about magic. He was working at a recording studio, and that seemed to be all he was concerned about.

The following year, life was the same. He quit his job and went to work at another studio.

During their third year together, he quit his job again (a mania for leaving everything behind!) and decided to write scripts for TV. She found it strange, the way he changed jobs every year—but he was writing, earning money, and they were living well.

Then, at the end of their third year together, he decided—once again—to quit his job. He gave no explanation, saying only that he was fed up with what he was doing, that it didn't make sense to keep quitting his jobs, changing one for another. He needed to discover what it was that he wanted. They had put some money aside, and had decided to do some traveling.

In a car, Chris thought, *just like we're doing now.*

❁

Chris had met J. for the first time in Amsterdam, when they were having coffee at a cafe in the

Brower Hotel, looking out at the Singel canal. Paulo had turned pale when he saw the tall, white-haired man dressed in a business suit. Despite his anxiety, he finally worked up the courage to approach the older man's table.

That night, when Paulo and Chris were alone again, he drank an entire bottle of wine. He wasn't a good drinker, and became drunk. Only then did he reveal what she already knew: that for seven years he had dedicated himself to learning magic. Then, for some reason—which he never explained, although she asked about it a number of times—he had given it all up.

"I had a vision of J. two months ago, when we visited Dachau," Paulo said.

Chris remembered that day. Paulo had wept. He said that he was being called but didn't know how to respond.

"Should I go back to magic?" he had asked.

"Yes, you should," she had answered, but she wasn't sure.

Since Amsterdam, everything had changed. There were rituals, exercises, practices. There were long trips with J., with no defined date of return. There were long meetings with strange women, and men who had an aura of sensuality about them. There were challenges and tests, long nights when he didn't sleep, and long weekends when he never left the house. But Paulo was much happier, and he no longer thought about quitting his job. Together they had founded a small publishing house, and he was doing something he'd dreamed of for a long time: writing books.

❋

Finally, a gas station. As a young Native American woman filled the tank, Paulo and Chris took a stroll.

Paulo looked at the map and confirmed the route. Yes, they were on the right road.

Now he can relax. Now he'll talk a bit, Chris thought.

"Did J. say you were to meet with your angel here?" she asked hesitantly.

"No," he replied.

Great, he gave me an answer, she thought, as she looked out at the brilliant green vegetation, lit by the setting sun. If she hadn't checked the map so often, she too would have doubted this was the right road. The map said that they should be at their destination in another six miles or so, but the scenery seemed to be telling them they had a long way to go.

"I didn't have to come here," Paulo continued. "Any place would do. But I have a contact here."

Of course. Paulo always had contacts. He referred to such people as members of the Tradition; but when Chris described them in her diary, she referred to them as the "Conspiracy." Among them were sorcerers and witch doctors—the kind of people one has nightmares about.

"Someone who speaks with angels?"

"I'm not sure. One time, J. referred—just in passing—to a master of the Tradition who lives here, and who knows how to communicate with the angels. But that might just be a rumor."

He might have been speaking seriously, but Chris knew that he might also have just selected a place at random, one of the many places where he had "contacts." A place that was far from their daily life, and where he could concentrate better on the Extraordinary.

"How are you going to speak to your angel?"

"I don't know," he replied.

What a strange way to live, thought Chris. She looked at her husband as he walked over to pay the bill. All she knew was that he felt he had to speak with the angels, and that was that! Drop everything, jump on a plane, fly for twelve hours from

Brazil to Los Angeles, drive for six hours to this gas station, arm himself with enough patience to remain here for forty days: all of this in order to speak—or rather, try to speak—with his guardian angel!

He laughed at her, and she smiled back. After all, this wasn't all that bad. They had their occasional daily irritations—paying bills, cashing checks, paying courtesy calls, accepting some tough times.

But they still believed in angels.

"We'll do it," she said.

"Thanks for the 'we,'" he answered with a smile. "But I'm the magus around here."

THE WOMAN AT THE STATION HAD SAID they were going in the right direction—about ten more minutes. They drove in silence. Paulo turned the radio off. There was a small elevation, but only when they reached the top did they realize how high up they were. They had been climbing steadily for six hours, without realizing it.

But they were there.

He parked on the shoulder and turned off the motor. Chris looked back in the direction from which they had come to see if it was true: Yes, she could see green trees, plants, vegetation.

But there in front of them, extending from horizon to horizon, was the Mojave Desert: the enormous desert that spreads into many states and into Mexico, the desert she had seen so many times in Westerns when she was a child, the desert that had places with strange names like the Rainbow Forest and Death Valley.

It's pink, Chris thought, but she didn't say anything. He was staring out at its immensity, trying to determine where the angels dwelt.

❀

If you stand in the middle of the main park, you can see where the town of Borrego Springs begins and where it ends. But there are three hotels for the winter tourists who come there for the sun.

They left their luggage in the room and went to a Mexican restaurant for dinner. The waiter stood nearby for some time, trying to determine what language they were speaking. Finally, when he couldn't figure it out, he asked. When they said they were from Brazil, he said he had never met a Brazilian before.

"Well, now you've met two," Paulo laughed.

By the next day, the entire town will have heard about it, he thought. *There's not much news in Borrego Springs.*

After their meal, they walked about the town, hand in hand. Paulo wanted to wander out into the desert, get the feel of it, breathe in the air of the Mojave. So they meandered over the desert's rocky floor for a half hour, at last stopping to look back at the few distant lights of Borrego Springs.

There in the desert, the heavens were clear. They sat on the ground and made their separate wishes on the falling stars. There was no moon, and the constellations stood out brilliantly.

"Have you ever had the feeling, at certain moments in your life, that someone was observing what you were doing?" Paulo asked Chris.

"How did you know that?"

"I just know. There are moments when, without really knowing it, we are aware of the presence of angels."

Chris thought back to her adolescence. In those days, she had had that feeling very strongly.

"At such moments," he continued, "we begin to create a kind of film in which we are the main character, and we are certain that someone is observing our actions.

"But then, as we get older, we begin to think that such things are ridiculous. We think of it as having been just a child's fantasy of being a movie actor. We forget that, at those moments in which we are presenting ourselves before an invisible audience, the sensation of being observed was very strong."

He paused for a moment.

"When I look up at the night sky, that feeling often returns, and my question is always the same: Who is out there watching us?"

"And who is it?"

"Angels. God's messengers."

She stared up at the heavens, wanting to believe what he had said.

"All religions, and every person who has ever

witnessed the Extraordinary, speak of angels," Paulo went on. "The universe is populated with angels. It's they who give us hope. Like the one who announced that the Messiah had been born. They also bring death, like the exterminating angel that traveled through Egypt destroying all those who did not display the right sign at their door. Angels with flaming swords in their hands can prevent us from entering into paradise. Or they can invite us in, as the angel did to Mary.

"Angels remove the seals placed on prohibited books, and they sound the trumpets on the day of Final Judgment. They bring the light, as Michael did, or darkness, as Lucifer did."

Hesitantly, Chris asked, "Do they have wings?"

"Well, I haven't seen an angel yet," he answered. "But I wondered about that, too. I asked J. about it."

That's good, she thought. *At least I'm not the only one who has simple questions about the angels.*

"J. said that they take whatever form a person imagines they have. Because they are God's thoughts in live form, and they need to adapt to our wisdom and our knowledge. They know that if they don't, we'll be unable to see them."

Paulo closed his eyes.

"Imagine your angel, and you will feel its presence right now, right here."

They fell quiet, lying there on the floor of the desert. There was not a sound to be heard, and Chris began once again to feel like she was in a film, playing to an invisible audience. The more intensely she concentrated, the more certain she was that all around her there was a strong presence, friendly and generous. She began to imagine her angel, dressed in blue, with golden hair and immense white wings—exactly as she had pictured her angel as a child.

Paulo was imagining his angel, as well. He had already immersed himself many times in the invisible world that surrounded them, so it was not a new experience for him. But now, since J. had assigned him this task, he felt that his angel was much more present—as if the angels made themselves available only to those who believed in their existence. He knew, though, that whether one believed in them or not, they were always there—messengers of life, of death, of hell, and of paradise.

He dressed his angel in a long robe, embroidered in gold. And he also gave his angel wings.

The hotel watchman, eating his breakfast, turned to them as they came in.

"I wouldn't go out into the desert at night again," he said.

This really is a small town, Chris thought. *Everybody knows what you're doing.*

"It's dangerous in the desert at night," the guard explained. "That's when the coyotes come out, and the snakes. They can't stand the heat of the day, so they do their hunting after the sun goes down."

"We were looking for our angels," Paulo said.

The watchman thought that the man didn't speak English very well. What he had said didn't make sense. Angels! Perhaps he'd meant something else.

The two finished their coffee quickly. Paulo's "contact" had set their meeting for early in the morning.

CHRIS WAS SURPRISED WHEN SHE SAW Gene for the first time. He was quite young, certainly not more than twenty, and he lived in a trailer out in the desert, several miles from Borrego Springs.

"This is a master of the Conspiracy?" she whispered to Paulo, when the youth had gone to fetch some iced tea.

But Gene was back before Paulo could respond. They sat under an awning that extended along the side of the trailer.

They talked about the rituals of the Templars, about reincarnation, about Sufi magic, about the Catholic church in Latin America. The boy seemed to know a great deal, and it was amusing to listen to their conversation—they sounded like fans discussing a popular sport, defending certain tactics and criticizing others.

They spoke of everything—except angels.

The heat of the day was intensifying. They drank more tea as Gene, smiling agreeably, told them of the marvels of the desert. He warned them that novices should never go into it at night, and that it would be smart to avoid the hottest hours of the day, as well.

"The desert is made of mornings and afternoons," he said. "The other times are risky."

Chris listened to their conversation for as long as she could. But she had awakened early, and the sun was getting stronger and stronger. She decided she'd close her eyes and take a quick nap.

WHEN SHE AWOKE, THE SOUND OF THEIR voices was coming from a different place. The two men were at the rear of the trailer.

"Why did you bring your wife?" she heard Gene ask in a guarded tone.

"Because I was coming to the desert," Paulo answered, also whispering.

Gene laughed.

"But you're missing what's best about the desert. The solitude."

What a cheeky kid, Chris thought.

"Tell me about the Valkyries you mentioned," Paulo said.

"They can help you to find your angel," replied Gene. "They're the ones who instructed me. But the Valkyries are jealous and tough. They try to follow the same rules as the angels—and, you know, in the kingdom of the angels, there is no good and no evil."

"Not as we understand them," Paulo countered.

Chris had no idea what they meant by "Valkyries." She had a vague memory of having heard the name in the title of an opera.

"Was it difficult for you to see your angel?"

"A better word would be *anguishing.* It happened all of a sudden, back in the days when the Valkyries came through here. I decided I'd learn the process just for the fun of it, because at that point, I didn't yet understand the language of the desert, and I was upset about everything that was happening to me.

"My angel appeared on that third mountain peak. I was up there just wandering and listening to music on my Walkman. In those days, I had already mastered the second mind."

What the hell is the "second mind"? Chris wondered.

"Was it your father who taught it to you?"

"No. And when I asked him why he had never told me about the angels, he told me that some things are so important that you have to learn about them on your own."

They were silent for a moment.

"If you meet with the Valkyries, there's something that will make it easier for you to get along with them," Gene said.

"What's that?"

The young man laughed.

"You'll find out. But it would have been a lot better if you hadn't brought your wife along."

"Did your angel have wings?" Paulo asked.

Before Gene could answer, Chris had arisen from her folding chair, come around the trailer, and now stood before them.

"Why is he making such a big thing about your coming here alone?" she asked, speaking Portuguese. "Do you want me to leave?"

Gene went on with what he was saying to Paulo, paying no attention whatsoever to Chris's interruption. She waited for Paulo's answer—but she might just as well have been invisible.

"Give me the keys to the car," she said, at the limit of her patience.

"What does your wife want?" Gene finally asked.

"She wants to know what the 'second mind' is."

Damn! Nine years we've been together, and this stranger already knows all about us!

Gene stood up.

"Sit down, close your eyes, and I will show you what the second mind is," he said.

"I didn't come here to the desert to learn about magic or converse with angels," Chris said. "I came only to be with my husband."

"Sit down," Gene insisted, smiling.

She looked at Paulo for a fraction of a second, but was unable to determine what he was thinking.

I respect their world, but it has nothing to do with me, she thought. Although all their friends thought that she had become completely involved in her husband's lifestyle, the fact was that she and he had spoken very little of it to one another. She was used to going with him to certain places, and had once even carried his sword for purposes of a ceremony. She knew the Road to Santiago, and had—because of their relationship—learned quite a bit about sexual magic. But that was all. J. had never proposed that he teach her anything.

"What should I do?" she asked Paulo.

"Whatever you think," he answered.

I love you, she thought. If she were to learn something about his world, there was no doubt it would bring them even closer. She went back to her chair, sat down, and closed her eyes.

"What are you thinking about?" Gene asked her.

"About what you two were discussing. About Paulo traveling by himself. About the second mind. Whether his angel has wings. And why this should interest me at all. I mean, I don't think I've ever spoken to angels."

"No, no. I want to know whether you're thinking about something else. Something beyond your control."

She felt his hands touching both sides of her head.

"Relax. Relax." His voice was gentle. "What are you thinking?"

There were sounds. And voices. It was only now that she realized what she was thinking, although it had been there for almost an entire day.

"A melody," she answered. "I've been singing this melody to myself ever since I heard it yesterday on the radio on our way here."

It was true, she had been humming the melody incessantly. To the end, and then once again, and then from start to finish again. She couldn't get it out of her mind.

Gene asked that she open her eyes.

"That's the second mind," he said. "It's your second mind that's humming the song. It can do that with anything. If you're in love with someone, you can have that person inside your head. The same thing happens with someone you want to forget about. But the second mind is a tough thing to deal with. It's at work regardless of whether you want it to be or not."

He laughed.

"A song! We're always impassioned about something. And it's not always a song. Have you ever had someone you loved stick in your mind? It's really terrible when that happens. You travel, you try to forget, but your second mind keeps saying: 'Oh, he would really love that!' 'Oh, if only he were here.'"

Chris was astonished. She had never thought of such a thing as a second mind.

She had two minds. Functioning at the same time.

GENE CAME TO HER SIDE.

"Close your eyes again," he said. "And try to remember the horizon you were looking at."

She tried to recall it. "I can't," she said, her eyes still closed. "I wasn't looking at the horizon. I know that it's all around me, but I wasn't looking at it."

"Open your eyes and look at it."

Chris looked out at the horizon. She saw mountains, rocks, stones, and sparse and spindly vegetation. A sun that shone brighter and brighter seemed to pierce her sunglasses and burn into her eyes.

"You are here," Gene said, now with a serious tone of voice. "Try to understand that you are here, and that the things that surround you change you—in the same way that you change them."

Chris stared at the desert.

"In order to penetrate the invisible world and develop your powers, you have to live in the present, the *here and now.* In order to live in the present, you have to control your second mind. And look at the horizon."

Gene asked her to concentrate on the melody that she had been humming. It was "When I Fall in Love." She didn't know the words, and had been making them up, or just singing a ta-de-dum.

Chris concentrated. In a few moments, the melody disappeared. She was now completely alert, listening only to Gene's words.

But Gene seemed to have nothing more to say.

"I have to be alone now," he said. "Come back in two days."

PAULO AND CHRIS LOCKED THEMSELVES inside their air-conditioned hotel room, unwilling to confront the 110 degrees of the midday desert. No books to read, nothing to do. They tried taking a nap, but couldn't sleep.

"Let's explore the desert," Paulo said.

"It's too hot out there. Gene said it was even dangerous. Let's do it tomorrow."

Paulo didn't answer. He was certain he could turn the fact that he was locked into his hotel room into a learning experience. He tried to make sense of everything that happened in his life, and used conversation only as means for discharging tension.

But it was impossible; trying to find a meaning in everything meant he had to remain alert and tense. Paulo never relaxed, and Chris had often asked herself when he would tire of his intensity.

"Who is Gene?"

"His father is a powerful magus, and he wants Gene to maintain the family tradition—like engineers who want their children to follow in their footsteps."

"He's young, but he wants to act mature," Chris commented. "And he's giving up the best years of his life out here in the desert."

"Everything has its price. If Gene goes through all this—and doesn't abandon the Tradition—he'll be the first in a line of young masters to be integrated into a world that the older masters, although they understand it, no longer know how to explain."

Paulo lay down and started to read the only book available, *The Guide to Lodging in the Mojave Desert*. He didn't want to tell his wife that, in addition to what he had already told her, there was another reason that Gene was here: He was powerful in the paranormal processes, and had been prepared by the Tradition to be ready to act when the gates to paradise opened.

Chris wanted to talk. She felt anxious cooped up in the hotel room, and had decided not to "make sense of everything," as her husband did. She was not there to seek a place within a community of the elite.

"I didn't really understand what Gene was trying to teach me," she said. "The solitude and the desert can increase your contact with the invisible world. But I think it causes us to lose contact with other people."

"He probably has a girlfriend or two around here," Paulo said, wanting to avoid conversation.

*If I have to spend another thirty-nine days locked up
with Paulo, I'll commit suicide,* she promised herself.

THAT AFTERNOON, THEY WENT TO A COFFEE shop across the street from the hotel. Paulo chose a table by the window. They ordered ice cream. Chris had spent several hours studying her second mind, and had learned to control it much better than before, but her appetite was never subject to control.

Paulo said, "I want you to pay close attention to the people who pass by."

She did as Paulo had asked. In the next half hour, only five people passed by.

"What did you see?"

She described the people in detail—their clothing, approximate age, what they were carrying. But apparently that wasn't what he wanted to hear. He insisted on more, trying to get a better answer, but couldn't do so.

"Okay," he said. "I'm going to tell you what it was that I wanted you to notice: All the people who passed by in the street were looking down."

They waited for some time before another person walked by. Paulo was right.

"Gene asked you to look to the horizon. Try that."

"What do you mean?"

"All of us create a kind of 'magic space' around us. Usually it's a circle with about a fifteen-foot radius, and we pay attention to what goes on within it. It doesn't matter whether it's people, tables, telephones, or windows; we try to maintain control over that small world that we, ourselves, create.

"A magus, though, always looks much further. We expand that 'magic space' and try to control a great many more things. They call it 'looking at the horizon.'"

"Well, why should I do that?"

"Because you're here. If you do it, you'll see how much things change."

When they left the coffee shop, she started to pay attention to things in the distance. She noticed the mountains, the occasional cloud that appeared as the sun began to set, and—in a strange way—she seemed to be seeing the air about her.

"Everything Gene told you is important," Paulo said. "He has already seen and talked with his angel, and he is using you as a means of instructing me. He knows the power of his words, and he knows that advice not heeded is returned to its giver, losing its energy. He needs to be sure that you are interested in what he tells you."

"Well, why doesn't he show these things directly to you?"

"Because there is an unwritten rule in the Tradition: A master never teaches another master's disciple. And he knows I am J.'s disciple. But since he wants to be of help to me, he is using you for that purpose."

"Is that why you brought me here?"

"No. It was because I was afraid of being alone in the desert."

He could have said it was because he loves me, she thought. *That would have been more truthful.*

THEY STOPPED THE CAR ON THE SHOULDER of the narrow dirt road. Two days had passed, and they were to meet Gene that night—Gene, who had told her always to look to the horizon. She was excited about their meeting.

But it was still morning. And the days in the desert were long.

She looked out at the horizon: mountains that suddenly sprang up millions of years ago, crossing the desert in a long *cordillera*. Although the earthquakes that created them had occurred long ago, one could still see how the earth's surface had buckled—the ground still climbed smoothly toward the mountains, and then, at a certain altitude, a kind of wound opened, out of which rocks sprang, pointing to the sky.

Between the mountains and the car was a rocky valley with sparse vegetation: thorn bushes, cacti, and yucca. Life that insisted on surviving in an environment that didn't support it. And an immense white expanse the size of five football fields stood out in the middle of it all. It reflected the morning sun, and resembled a field of snow.

"Salt. A salt lake."

Yes. This desert must once have been the bed of an ocean. Once a year, seagulls from the Pacific

Ocean flew the hundreds of miles to this desert to eat the species of shrimp that appeared when the rains began. Human beings may forget their origins, but nature, never.

"It must be about three miles from here," Chris said.

Paulo checked his watch. It was still early. They had looked to the horizon and it had shown them a salt lake. One hour's walk there, another to return, no risk of the midday sun.

Each placed a canteen of water on their belt. Paulo put his cigarettes and a Bible in a small bag. When they arrived at the lake, he was going to suggest that they read a passage from it, chosen at random.

THEY BEGAN TO WALK. CHRIS KEPT HER eyes fixed on the horizon whenever possible. Although it was a simple thing to be doing, something strange was happening: She felt better, freer, as if her internal energy had been increased. For the first time in many years, she regretted not having taken a more intense interest in Paulo's "Conspiracy." She had always imagined difficult rituals that only those who were prepared and disciplined could perform.

They walked at a leisurely pace for half an hour. The lake appeared to have shifted its location; it always seemed to be at the same distance from them.

They walked for another hour. They must already have covered four miles or so, but the lake appeared to be only a bit closer.

It was no longer early morning, and the heat of the sun was building.

Paulo looked back. He could see the car, a tiny red point in the distance but still visible—impossible to become lost. And when he looked at the car, he saw something else that was important.

"Let's stop here," he said.

They left the path they were taking and walked to a boulder. They huddled in close to it, because it

42

cast only a very small shadow. In the desert, shadows appear only early in the morning or late in the afternoon, and then only near the rocks.

"Our calculation was wrong," he said.

Chris had already noticed that. She was surprised, because Paulo was good at estimating distances, and he had trusted her guess of three or four miles.

"I know how we went wrong," he said. "There's nothing in the desert to base comparisons on. We're used to calculating distance based on the size of things. We know the approximate size of a tree, or a telephone pole, or a house. They help us to decide whether things are near or far away."

Here, there was no point of reference. There were rocks they'd never seen, mountains whose size they could not estimate, and only the sparse vegetation. Paulo had realized this as he looked back at the car. And he could see that they had walked more than four miles.

"Let's rest a while, and then we'll go back."

That's all right, Chris thought. She was fascinated with the idea of continuing to look out at the horizon. It was a completely new experience for her.

"This business of looking at the horizon, Paulo . . ." Chris paused.

He waited, knowing that she would continue. He knew that she was worried that she might say something silly, or find some esoteric meaning in things, as many do who know only a little about the path.

"It seems as if . . . I don't know . . . I can't explain it . . . as if my soul has grown."

Yes, Paulo thought. *She's on the right track.*

"Before, I looked in the distance, and things in the distance seemed really *far,* you know? They seemed not to be a part of my world. Because I was used to looking only at things that were close, the things around me.

"But, two days ago, I got used to looking into the distance. And I saw that besides tables, chairs, and objects, my world also included the mountains, clouds, the sky. And my soul—my soul seems to have eyes that it uses to touch those things."

Wow! That's a great way of saying it, Paulo thought.

"My soul seems to have grown," Chris repeated.

He opened the bag, took out his cigarettes, and lit one before speaking.

"Anyone can see that. But we're always looking at the things that are closest to us. Looking down and inward. So our power diminishes, and using your term, our soul shrinks.

"Because our soul includes nothing but ourselves. It doesn't include oceans, mountains, other people; it doesn't even include the walls of the houses where we live."

Paulo liked the expression "My soul has grown." If he had been talking with another member of the Tradition, there's no doubt that he would have heard much more complicated explanations, such as "My consciousness expanded." But the term his wife had used was more exact.

He finished his cigarette. There was no point in insisting that they make it to the lake; the temperature would soon reach 110 in the shade. The car was far away, but visible, and in an hour and a half they'd be back to it.

They started walking. Surrounded by the desert, by the huge horizon, a feeling of freedom began to grow in their souls.

"Let's take off our clothes," Paulo said.

"But someone might be watching," Chris said automatically.

Paulo laughed. They could see for miles around them. The day before, when they had been out walking all morning and afternoon, only two cars had passed—and, even then, they had heard the sound of their approach long before the cars had appeared. The desert was the sun, the wind, and the silence.

"Only our angels are watching," he answered. "And they've already seen us naked many times."

He took off his shorts and his shirt and the canteen, placing them all in the bag.

Chris struggled to keep from laughing. She took her clothes off too, and in a few moments they were two people crossing the Mojave in their sneakers, their hats, and their sunglasses—one of them carrying a bag. Anyone watching would find it hilarious.

THEY WALKED FOR HALF AN HOUR. THE car was still just a point on the horizon, but—in contrast to the lake—it was growing in size as they approached it. They would be there in a short while.

Suddenly, Chris felt tremendously tired.

"Let's rest for a few minutes," she said.

Paulo stopped immediately, saying, "I can't carry this bag anymore. I'm really tired."

How could he not be able to carry the bag? Even with everything it held, it couldn't weigh more than six or seven pounds.

"You have to carry it. The water's in there."

Right, he had to carry it.

"Well then, let's get going," he said irritably.

Everything was so romantic just a few minutes ago, thought Chris. And now he was irritated. Well, forget it. She was tired, too.

They walked a bit farther, and their exhaustion worsened. If it were up to her, nothing more would be said—she didn't want to make things worse.

What a dope, she thought. To get angry in the midst of such beauty, and right after they had been talking about such interesting things as . . .

She couldn't remember, but it wasn't important. She was too tired to think now.

Paulo stopped and put the bag down in the sand.

"Let's rest," he said.

He didn't seem irritated now. He must be getting tired, too. Just like her.

There was no shade. But she needed to rest.

They sat down on the hot sand. The fact that they were naked and that the ground burned their skin didn't matter. They had to stop. Just for a while.

She remembered what they had been discussing: horizons. She noticed that now, even without wanting to, she had the feeling that her soul had grown. And it seemed like her second mind had stopped working altogether. She didn't think of melodies or repetitious things, and she didn't even care if someone was watching them walk naked across the desert.

Nothing was important. She felt relaxed, unworried, free.

They sat there for a few minutes in silence. It was hot, but the sun didn't bother them. If it started to, they had plenty of water.

He stood up first.

"I think we had better keep walking. It's not far to the car now. We'll rest in the air-conditioning when we get there."

She was sleepy. She just wanted to nap for a bit. But she got up, anyway.

They walked a bit farther, and now the car was getting close. Not more than ten minutes to walk.

"Since we're so close, let's sleep for a while. Five minutes."

Sleep for five minutes? Why would he say that? Was he reading her mind? There couldn't be any problem with sleeping for just five minutes. They could get a good tan, as if they'd been to the beach.

They sat down again. They had been walking for half an hour, not counting their pauses. Why couldn't they just sleep for five minutes or so?

They heard the sound of a motor. Half an hour earlier, she would have leaped up and dressed in a hurry. But now, so what? It didn't matter at all. Let anyone look who wants to look. It didn't make any difference to her. She just wanted to sleep.

Paulo and Chris watched calmly as a truck drove down the road, passed their car, and stopped just beyond. A man got out and walked toward the vehicle. He looked inside, then walked around the car, examining everything.

Might be a thief, Paulo thought. He imagined the guy stealing the car, leaving them both stranded in the desert with no way to get back. The key was in the ignition—he hadn't taken it with him for fear of losing it.

But they were in the Mojave Desert. In New York, maybe. But here—no one stole cars here.

Chris looked out at the desert. It was golden and beautiful. Golden. Different from the pinkness of the desert at sundown.

An agreeable feeling of relaxation permeated her entire body. The sun didn't bother her—people didn't know how lovely the desert could be during the day!

The man gave up his inspection of the car, and placed his hand above his eyes. He was looking for them.

She was naked ... and he would surely see that. So what? Paulo didn't seem worried, either.

The man began walking toward them. The feeling of lightness and euphoria was increasing, but exhaustion kept them from moving. The desert was golden and beautiful. Everything was serene, at peace—the angels, yes, the angels would appear before long. That was what they had come to the desert for—to talk with their angels!

She was naked, and she was not ashamed.

The man stopped when he reached them. What

language was he speaking? They couldn't under-stand what he was saying.

Paulo tried to concentrate on what he was hear-ing, and realized that the man was speaking Eng-lish. After all, they were in the United States.

"Come with me," the man said.

"We want to rest," Paulo said. "Five minutes."

The man picked up the bag and opened it.

"Put this on," he said to Chris, handing her clothing to her.

She forced herself to get up, and did as he said. She was too tired to argue.

He ordered Paulo to do the same, and Paulo was also too tired to argue. The man saw the can-teens filled with water, opened one of them, filled the cap, and ordered them to drink.

They weren't thirsty. But they did as the man said. They were quite calm, and completely at peace with the world—and they had no desire to argue.

They would do anything they were told to do, obey any order, so long as they were left in peace.

"Let's walk," the man said.

They couldn't even think. They sat there gaz-ing at the desert. They would do anything so long as the stranger left them alone.

But the man escorted them to the car, told them to get in, and started the engine. "I wonder where he's taking us," Paulo thought. But he wasn't worried—the world was at peace, and the only thing he wanted to do was sleep. Surely his angel would appear before long.

PAULO AWOKE WITH HIS STOMACH churning, and a tremendous need to vomit.

"Lie still for a while longer."

Someone was speaking to him, but in his head there was only confusion. He still remembered the golden paradise where all had been serene and peaceful.

He tried to move, and felt as if thousands of needles were sticking into his head.

I think I'll go back to sleep, he thought. But he couldn't—the needles wouldn't allow it. And his stomach was still turning over.

"I want to throw up," he said.

When he opened his eyes, he saw that he was sitting in a kind of mini-market: He could see several refrigerator cabinets with soft drinks and shelves with foodstuffs. The sight of the food made him feel nauseated again. Then he noticed nearby a man he had never seen before.

The man helped him to get up. In addition to the imaginary needles in his head, Paulo realized that he had another in his arm. Only this one was real.

The man held the needle in place and helped Paulo to the bathroom, where he vomited some water, nothing more.

"What's happening? What's this needle for?"

It was Chris, speaking Portuguese. He returned to the store and saw that she was sitting up, too, with a needle in her arm.

Paulo felt a little better now, and no longer needed the man's support. He helped Chris up and to the bathroom, where she vomited.

"I'm going to use your car to get back to mine," the stranger said. "I'll leave the keys in the ignition. You can get a ride to it when you're ready."

Paulo was starting to remember what had happened, but the nausea had returned, and he had to vomit again.

When he came back, the man had left, but a boy of seventeen or eighteen was there.

"Just another hour," the boy said. "The solution will be used up then, and you can go."

"What time is it?"

The boy told them. Paulo struggled to get up—he had an appointment, and there was no way he was going to miss it.

"I have to meet with Gene," he said to Chris.

"Sit down," the boy said. "Not until the solution is used up."

The comment was unnecessary. Paulo no longer

had either the strength or desire to walk even to the door.

I've missed the meeting, he thought. But at this point, nothing mattered. The less he thought about, the better.

"FIFTEEN MINUTES," GENE SAID. "THAT'S all it takes, and without even realizing what's happening, you die."

They were back at the old trailer. It was the afternoon of the next day, and the entire scene was bathed in pink. Nothing like the desert of the previous day—golden, peaceful, nausea, vomiting.

They hadn't been able to eat or sleep for twenty-four hours—they threw up everything they tried to eat. But now that strange sensation was passing.

"It's good that your horizon had been expanded. And that you were thinking about angels. An angel appeared."

Paulo thought it would be better to have said "Your soul had grown." Besides, the guy who had appeared wasn't an angel—he had an old truck, and he spoke English.

"Let's get going," said Gene, asking Paulo to start the car. He took the passenger seat, with no show of ceremony. And Chris, grumbling in Portuguese, climbed into the back.

Gene began to give instructions—take that road there, go for a few miles, drive fast so that the car gets cool inside, turn off the air-conditioning so the motor doesn't overheat. Several times they drove off the narrow dirt road into the desert. But Gene knew what he was doing. He wasn't going to make the same mistakes they had.

"What happened yesterday?" Chris asked for the hundredth time. She knew that Gene wanted her to ask. He might already have seen his guardian angel, but he acted like any other young man his age.

"Sunstroke," he finally explained. "Haven't either of you ever seen a film about the desert?"

Of course they had. Thirsty men, dragging themselves across the sand in search of a drop of water.

"We didn't feel thirsty at all. The two canteens were filled with water."

"That's not what I'm talking about," the American interrupted. "I mean your clothing."

The clothing! The Arabs with their long robes, and several hoods—one on top of the other. Of course, how stupid we were! Paulo had already heard about that, and he'd already walked across three other deserts . . . and he had never felt the desire to take his clothes off. But here, that morning, after the frustration of the lake that they seemed never to reach. . . . *How could I have had such a stupid idea?* he thought.

"When you took off your clothes, the water in your bodies began to evaporate immediately. You can't even perspire, because the climate is so dry. In fifteen minutes, you were both already dehydrated. No thirst or anything—just a slight feeling of disorientation."

"And the exhaustion?"

"That exhaustion is death arriving."

I sure didn't know it was death arriving, Chris said to herself. If someday she had to choose an easy way to leave the world behind, she would come back and take off her clothing in the middle of the desert.

"Most people who die in the desert die with water in their canteen. The dehydration is so rapid that we feel as if we've drunk an entire bottle of whisky, or taken an overdose of some tranquilizer." He suggested that, starting now, they drink water periodically—even if they weren't thirsty—because their bodies needed the water.

"But an angel did appear," Gene said.

Before Paulo could say what he was thinking, Gene ordered him to stop at the foot of a cliff.

"Let's get out here and go the rest of the way on foot."

They began to walk along a narrow path that led to the top of the cliff. Before they had gone far, Gene realized he had forgotten the flashlight from the car. He went back, picked it up, and sat on the hood of the car for some time, staring out at the desert.

Chris is right; solitude does strange things to people. He's behaving strangely, Paulo thought as he watched the youth down below.

But, a few seconds later, Gene had climbed the narrow path again, and they pushed on.

In forty minutes, with no great difficulty, they had reached the top. There was some sparse vegetation there, and Gene asked that they sit down facing north. His attitude, usually expansive, had changed—he seemed more distant, and looked as if he were concentrating hard.

"You've both come here in search of angels," he said, sitting down at their side.

"That's what I came for," Paulo said. "And I know that you have spoken with one."

"Forget about my angel. Many people in this desert have already seen or conversed with their angel. So have a lot of people in cities, or at sea, or in the mountains."

There was a tone of impatience in his voice.

"Think about *your* guardian angels," he continued. "Because my angel is here, and I can see him. This is my holy place."

Both Paulo and Chris thought back to their first night in the desert. And they imagined their angels once again, with their raiment and their wings.

"You must always have a holy place. Mine once was a small apartment, and at another time, a square in the middle of Los Angeles. Now it's here. A sacred hymn opens a gate to heaven, and heaven appears."

They both looked around at Gene's holy place: the rocks, the hard ground, the desert plants. Perhaps snakes and coyotes passed through here at night, too.

Gene appeared to be in a trance.

"It was here that I was first able to see my angel, although I knew that the angel was everywhere, and that the angel's face is the face of the desert I live in, or of the city where I lived for eighteen years.

"I was able to talk with my angel because I had faith that the angel existed. And because I loved my angel."

Neither Chris nor Paulo dared ask what they had talked about.

Gene went on, "Everyone can make contact with four different kinds of entities in the invisible world: the elementals, the disembodied spirits, the saints, and the angels.

"The elementals are the vibrations of things in nature—fire, earth, water, and air—and we make contact with them using rituals. These are pure forces—like earthquakes, lightning, or volcanoes. Because we need to understand them as 'beings,' they traditionally appear in the form of dwarfs, fairies, or salamanders. But all one can do is use the power of the elementals—we never learn anything from them."

Why is he saying all this? Paulo thought. *Has he forgotten that I'm a master of magic, too?*

Gene continued his explanation, "The disembodied spirits are those that wander between one life and another, and we make contact with them by means of a medium. Some are great masters— but all that they teach us we can learn on earth, because that's where they learned what they know. Better, then, to let them wander in the direction of their next step, to look out at the horizon, and to take from *here* the same wisdom as they did."

Paulo must know all about this, Chris thought. *He's probably talking to me.*

❀ ❀ ❀

YES, GENE WAS SPEAKING TO CHRIS—IT was because she was here that he was here. There was nothing he could teach Paulo, twenty years older than he and more experienced, and who, on his own, would surely find the way to talk with his angel. Paulo was one of J.'s disciples—and the things Gene had heard about J.! At their first meeting, Gene had tried in various ways to get the Brazilian to talk, but the woman had made it impossible. He was unable to learn anything about the techniques, the processes, or the rituals used by J.

That first meeting had been deeply disappointing for him. He thought that the Brazilian might be using J.'s name without the master's knowledge. Or—who knows?—perhaps J. had made a mistake for the first time in his selection of a disciple. And if that were the case, the entire Tradition would soon know about it. But that night of their meeting, he had dreamed of his guardian angel.

And his angel had asked that he initiate the woman into the path of magic. Just initiate her: Her husband would do the rest.

In the dream, he argued that he had already taught her about the second mind, and had asked that she look out at the horizon. The angel said that Gene should pay attention to the man, but that he should take care of the woman. And then the angel disappeared.

Gene was trained to be disciplined. So he was now doing what the angel had commanded—and he hoped that it was being observed up above.

❁

"After the disembodied spirits," he continued, "the saints appear. These are the true masters. They lived among us at one time, and are now closer to the light. The great teachings of the saints are their lives here on earth. Contained in them are all we need to know, and all we have to do is imitate them."

"How do we invoke the saints?" Chris asked.

"Through prayer," Paulo answered, cutting Gene off.

He wasn't jealous—although it was clear to him that the American wanted to impress Chris. *He respects the Tradition. He's going to use my wife as a means of reaching me. But why is he being so basic, talking about things that I already know so well?* he thought.

"We invoke the saints through constant prayer," Paulo continued. "And when they are near, everything changes. Miracles happen."

Gene couldn't help but notice the Brazilian's hostile, almost aggressive tone of voice. But he wasn't going to say anything about his dream of the angel, because he didn't owe this man anything.

"Finally," Gene said, "there are the angels."

Perhaps Paulo didn't know about this part, even though he seemed to know many other things. Gene paused for a few moments. He sat there silently praying, and remembered his angel, and hoped that he was hearing every word. And he asked that his angel help him to be clear, because—my God!—it was so difficult to explain.

"Angels are love in motion. They never rest, they struggle to grow, and they are beyond good and evil. Love that consumes all, that destroys all, that forgives all. Angels are made of that love, and are at the same time its messengers.

"The love of the exterminating angel, who one day will take away our soul, and of the guardian angel, who brings our soul back. Love in motion."

"Love at war," Chris said.

"There is no love in peace. Whoever seeks peace is lost."

What does a boy like this know about love? He lives alone in the desert, and has never been in love, Chris thought. Meanwhile, no matter how hard she tried, she could think of not one moment when love had ever brought her peace. It was always accompanied by agony, intense joy, and deep sadness.

Gene turned to them. "Let's be silent for a while, so that our angels can hear the love that exists beyond our silence."

Chris was still thinking about love. Yes, the boy seemed to be right, although she could swear that all of his knowledge was theoretical. *Love comes to rest only when we are close to death. How strange.* How strange was everything that she was experiencing, especially the sensation that her soul had grown.

She had never asked Paulo to teach her anything—she believed in God, and that was sufficient. She respected her husband's search, but—perhaps because she was so close to him, or because she knew that he had the same defects as other men—she had never taken an interest in it.

But she didn't know Gene. He had said: "Try to look at the horizon. Pay attention to your second mind." And she had done so. Now, with her soul that had grown, she was discovering how good it was, and how much time she had wasted before.

"Why do we need to speak with our angels?" Chris asked, breaking the silence.

"To discover through them," replied Gene.

Gene wasn't bothered by the comment. If she had asked the question of Paulo, he would have been angry.

They said an Our Father and a Hail Mary. Then the American said that they could go back down.

"That's it?" Paulo asked, disappointed.

"I wanted to bring you here so my angel could see that I had done as my angel asked," Gene answered. "I have nothing else to teach you. If you want to learn more, seek out the Valkyries."

THEY MADE THE RETURN TRIP IN AWKWARD silence, interrupted only when Gene had to indicate which turn should be taken. No one was interested in conversation—Paulo, because he thought that Gene had tricked him; Chris, because Paulo might be irritated at her comments, feeling that she was spoiling everything; and Gene, because he knew that the Brazilians were disappointed, and because of this, would not talk about J. and his techniques.

"You are wrong about one thing," Paulo said when they arrived at the trailer. "It was not an angel that we met up with yesterday. It was a guy driving a truck."

For a fraction of a second, Chris thought there would be no response—the hostility between the two men was growing stronger and stronger. The American turned and began to walk in the direction of his home, but suddenly he stopped.

"I want to tell you a story my father told me," he said. "A master and his disciple were walking together in the desert. The master was teaching his charge that he could always trust in God, since he was aware of everything.

"Night fell, and they decided to pitch camp. The master raised the tent, and the disciple was given the assignment of tethering the horses to a rock. But, as he stood by the rock, he thought to himself: *The master is testing me. He said that God is aware of everything, and then asked me to tie up the horses. He wants to see whether or not I believe in God.*

"Instead of tethering the animals, he said a long prayer, and left the fate of the horses in God's hands.

"Next day, when they awoke, the horses were gone. Disappointed, the disciple complained to the master, saying that he no longer believed in him, since God had not taken care of everything, and had forgotten to watch over the horses.

"'You are wrong,' the master answered. 'God wanted to take care of the horses. But in order to do so, he needed to make use of your hands to tether them to the stone.'"

THE YOUNG MAN LIT A SMALL GAS lantern that was hanging outside the trailer. The light dimmed the brilliance of the stars somewhat.

"When we begin to think about our angels, they begin to manifest themselves. Their presence becomes closer and closer, more real. But, at the beginning, angels show themselves as they have done throughout our life: through others.

"Your angel used that man. He must have been caused to leave his home early—something must have changed in his routine, altering everything so that he could be there just at the moment that you needed him. That is a miracle. Do not try to regard it as a common event."

Paulo said nothing.

"Look," Gene explained. "When we were climbing the mountain, I forgot the flashlight," Gene went on. "You probably noticed that I was back at the car for quite a while. Whenever I forget something on leaving the house, I feel that my guardian angel is in action, causing me to lose a few seconds—and this short time interval may signify important things. It may allow me to avoid an accident, or cause me to run into someone I need to see.

"So, after I get what I've forgotten, I always sit down and count to twenty. That way, the angel has time to take action. An angel uses many instruments."

Gene asked Paulo to wait where he was for a few moments. He entered the trailer, and returned with a map. "The last time I saw the Valkyries, it was here."

He pointed to a place on the map. Chris realized that the animosity between the two seemed to have lessened.

"Take care of her," Gene said. "It's a good thing that she came with you."

"I think so," Paulo said. "Thank you for everything."

And they said good-bye.

"WHAT A FOOL I'VE BEEN," PAULO SAID, punching the steering wheel as they drove away.

"What do you mean, a fool? I thought you were jealous!"

But Paulo was laughing, in a good mood.

"Four processes! And he only said three! It's through the fourth process that you converse with your angel!"

He looked at Chris, and his eyes were gleaming with the joy of discovery.

"The fourth process: channeling!"

ALMOST TEN DAYS IN THE DESERT. THEY stopped at one place where the ground had opened in a series of wounds, as if prehistoric rivers had run through there, dozens of them, leaving long, deep arroyos that were becoming larger through the action of the sun.

In those parts, not even the scorpions could survive, much less snakes, coyotes, or the ever-present tumbleweed. The desert was full of such places, known as badlands.

The two entered into one of the immense wounds. The earthen walls were high, and all that could be seen was a tortuous path, with no beginning or end.

They were no longer irresponsible adventurers, feeling that nothing could harm them. The desert had its laws, and killed those who did not respect them. They had learned what the laws were—the sound of the rattlesnake, the hours that it was safe to be out there, the precautions. Before entering the badlands, they had left a note in the car saying where they were going. Even if it were only for half an hour, and it appeared to be unnecessary, ridiculous, a car might stop, and someone would see the note and know what direction they had taken. They had to facilitate the instruments of their guardian angels.

They were looking for the Valkyries. Not there, at the end of the world—because nothing living could survive for long in those badlands. There—well, this was just training. For Chris.

But they knew that the Valkyries were nearby, because they saw the signs. They lived in the desert, never staying for long in one place—but they left signs.

Paulo and Chris had found some clues. At the beginning, they had stopped at one small town after another, asking about the Valkyries, and no one had ever heard of them. The directions Gene had given them were of no use—they had probably long ago passed by the spot on the map he had shown them. But one day, in a bar, they met a boy who remembered having read something about them. He described the way the Valkyries dressed, and the signs they left.

They began to ask others about women who were dressed that way. Some responded with obvious disapproval, saying the Valkyries had passed by a month ago, a week ago, three days ago.

Finally, they had reached a place that seemed to be just a day's travel from where the Valkyries should be.

THE SUN WAS ALREADY NEAR THE horizon—or they would not have risked being out in the desert. The earthen walls cast shadows. It was the perfect place.

Chris couldn't stand to repeat the whole thing yet again. But she had to—she hadn't yet achieved any meaningful results.

"Sit there. With your back to the sun."

She did as Paulo said. And then, automatically, she began to relax. She sat cross-legged, with her eyes closed—but she could feel the entire desert surrounding her. Her soul had been swelling during these days in the desert, and she knew that her world had expanded. It was more vast than it had been two weeks earlier.

"Concentrate on your second mind," he said.

Chris sensed an inhibited tone in his voice. He could not act toward her in the same way as he did with other disciples—after all, she knew his faults and weaknesses. But Paulo made a supreme effort to act as a master would, and she respected him for that.

She concentrated on her second mind. She allowed all thoughts to come to mind—and, as always, they were absurd thoughts for someone who was in the middle of the desert. For the past three days, whenever she had tried the exercise, she realized that her automatic thinking was very much concerned with whom she should invite to her birthday celebration—three months from now.

But Paulo had asked that she not be concerned about that. That she allow her concerns to flow freely.

"Let's start from the beginning again," he said.

"I'm thinking about my party."

"Don't fight your thoughts. They are stronger than you are," Paulo said for the thousandth time. "If you want to rid yourself of them, accept them. Think about what they want you to think about until they grow tired."

She went over her list of invitations. She rejected some. She substituted others. This was the first step: Pay attention to the second mind until it grew tired.

Now, the birthday celebration disappeared more quickly than before. But she was still composing the list. It was unbelievable how a subject like that could demand her attention for so many days, occupy hours when she could be thinking of more interesting things.

"Think until you are tired. Then, when you are tired, open the channel."

Paulo walked away from his wife and leaned against the wall. Gene was an expert, and took very seriously the business of not being able to teach anything to the disciple of another master. But, through Chris, he had given Paulo all of the clues that he needed.

The fourth way of communicating with the invisible world was channeling.

Channeling! How many times had he seen people in their cars in the midst of a traffic snarl, talking to themselves, without realizing that they were performing one of the most sophisticated of the magical processes! But, because of its extreme simplicity, all one need do is sit in a quiet place and be attentive to the thoughts that emerge from the bottom of one's mind.

Channeling has generally been considered a superficial practice. Nothing of the kind! Since the beginnings of humanity, people have known that, if they wanted to enter into contact with God, they had to make room in their soul. They had to allow their spiritual energy to manifest itself, and to create a bridge between the visible and the invisible.

How can one create such a bridge? Various mystical processes address the importance of "not being." Relax, allow the mind to become empty, and surprise yourself with the great treasure that begins to flow from your soul. The word *inspiration* means exactly that: the bringing in of air, allowing oneself to drink from an unknown source.

Channeling required no loss of awareness during the contact with the spirits; it was a more natural process for a person to use in order to plunge into the unknown. It allowed for contact with the Holy Spirit, with the soul of the world, with the enlightened masters. No ritual was needed, no incorporation, nothing. Every human being knew, subconsciously, that there was a bridge available to the invisible, a bridge one could cross without fear.

And everyone tried to do so, even without being aware of it. Everyone surprised themselves, saying things they had never thought before, giving advice of the "I don't know why I'm saying this" type, doing certain things that didn't appear to make sense.

And everyone liked to spend time observing nature's miracles—a thunderstorm, a sunset—ready to enter into contact with the universal wisdom, think about things that were truly important.

But at such times, the invisible wall would appear: the second mind.

The second mind was there, barring the entrance, with its repetitive ideas, its unimportant problems, its melodies, its financial problems, its unresolved passions.

He stood and approached Chris.

"Be patient, and listen to everything your second mind has to say. Don't respond. Don't argue. It will get tired."

Once again, Chris went over the invitation list, even though she had already lost interest in it. When she finished, she put a period to it.

And she opened her eyes.

There she was, in that wound in the earth. She felt the still air that surrounded her.

"Open the channel. Begin to speak."

Speak!

She had always been fearful of speaking out, of seeming ridiculous, stupid. Fearful of learning what others thought of what she said, because they always seemed more capable, more intelligent. Always seemed to have an answer for everything.

But now she was here, and she had to have the courage even to say things that made no sense, that were absurd. Paulo had explained that this was one way of channeling: speak. Conquer your second mind, and allow the universe to do what it wanted with it.

She began to move her head back and forth, wanting to do all that, and suddenly she wanted to make strange noises. And she did so. It wasn't ridiculous. She was free to do as she pleased.

She had no idea where these things came from—but they were coming from within, from the bottom of her soul, and manifesting themselves. From time to time, her second mind returned with its concerns, and Chris tried to organize them, but that's the way it had to be—no logic, no censure, but rather the joy of a warrior entering into an unknown world. She needed to speak the pure language of the heart.

Paulo listened in silence, and Chris felt his presence. She was totally aware, but free. She could not concern herself with what he was thinking—she had to continue to speak, making the gestures that came to her, singing the strange melodies. Yes, everything must make some kind of sense, because she had never heard these sounds before, these melodies, these words and movements. It was difficult, and she had the fear that she was fantasizing things, wanting to appear to be more in contact with the Invisible than she really was. But she overcame her fear of the ridiculous, and went on.

Today, something different was happening. She was no longer doing what she did out of obligation, as in the first days. She was enjoying herself. And she began to feel secure. A wave of security washed back and forth, and Chris tried desperately to go with it.

In order to keep the wave close to her, she had to speak. Say anything that came to mind.

"I see the earth." Her voice was hesitant, calm, even though her second mind made an appearance from time to time, saying that Paulo must be finding all of this ridiculous. "We are in a safe place, we can stay here tonight, lie here and look up at the stars and talk of angels. There are no scorpions, no snakes, no coyotes.

"The planet set aside certain places for itself. It tells us to go away. In those places, without the millions of life forms that walk on its surface, the earth is able to be alone. She also needs her solitude, for she needs to understand herself."

Why am I saying that? He's going to think I'm showing off. I'm aware!

Paulo looked around. The dry bed of the river seemed gentle, smooth. But it inspired a terror of total solitude, of the complete absence of life.

"Say a prayer," Chris went on. Her second mind was no longer able to make her feel ridiculous.

But suddenly, she felt fear. Fear of not knowing which prayer, of not knowing how to continue.

And when she felt the fear, her second mind returned—and the ridicule, the shame, the concern about Paulo returned with it. After all, he was the Magus—he knew more than she, and must think all of this was phony.

She took a deep breath. She concentrated on the present, on the earth where nothing grew, on the sun that was already hidden. Bit by bit, the wave of security came back—like a miracle.

"Say a prayer," she repeated.

> And it is going to echo
> clearly
> against the sky
> when I come along
> making my noise

She sat there in silence for a while, sensing that she had given her all, and that the channeling had ended. Then she turned to him.

"I went very far today. It's never happened that way."

Paulo caressed her face and kissed her. She didn't know whether he was doing that out of pity or pride.

"Let's go," he said. "Let's respect the earth's desire."

"Maybe he is saying that to give me a stimulus, to get me to try to continue channeling," she thought. But she was certain—something had happened. She hadn't invented all that.

"The prayer?" she asked, fearful of his answer.

"It's an ancient indigenous chant. From the Ojibway shamans."

She was proud of her husband's knowledge, even though he said it didn't count for much.

"How can these things happen?"

Paulo remembered J., discussing in his book the secrets of alchemy: "The clouds are rivers that already know the sea." But he wasn't inclined to explain. He was feeling tense, irritable, and didn't know exactly why he was staying on in the desert; after all, he already knew how to converse with his guardian angel.

"Did you see the film *Psycho?*" Paulo asked Chris when they arrived back at the car.

Chris nodded her head.

"The lead actress dies in the bathroom early on in the film. In the desert, I learned how one converses with the angels by the third day. Meanwhile, I promised myself that I would spend forty days here, and now I can't change my mind."

"Well, there's still the Valkyries."

"The Valkyries! I can live without them!"

He's afraid that he won't succeed in finding them, Chris thought.

"I already know how to converse with the angels, and that's what's important." Paulo's tone of voice was hostile.

"I've been thinking about that," Chris answered. "You already know, *but you don't want to try.*"

That's my problem, Paulo said to himself as he started the car. *I need some strong emotions. I need a challenge.*

He looked over at Chris. She was busy reading *The Desert Survival Manual* they had bought in one of the towns they had passed through. They drove off through yet another of the immense desert flats that seemed to have no end.

It's not just a problem of spiritual search, he continued thinking, as he alternated between looking at
Chris and watching the road. He loved his wife, but
he was getting fed up with marriage. He needed
some strong passion in his love, in his work, in almost everything he did in his life. And that went
against one of nature's most important laws: Every
movement needs to pause at times.

He knew that if he continued the way he was,
nothing in his life would last for very long. He was
beginning to understand what J. had meant when
he said that people wind up killing what they love
most.

Two days later, they reached Gringo Pass, a place with only one motel, a mini-market, and the U.S. customs building. The Mexican border was only a few yards from the center of town, and the two took snapshots of each other with one foot in each country.

At the mini-market, they asked about the Valkyries, and the woman who owned the luncheonette said she had seen "that bunch of lesbians" that morning, but that they had moved on.

"Did they cross into Mexico?" Paulo asked.

"No, no. They took the road to Tucson."

They went back to the motel, and sat down on the verandah. The car was parked directly in front of them.

"Look how dirty the car's become," Paulo said after a few minutes. "I think I'll wash it."

"The owner of the motel wouldn't like to find out people are using water for washing their car. We're in the desert, remember?"

Paulo didn't answer. He stood up, took a roll of paper towels from the car, and began to wipe away at the dust. Chris remained seated.

He's upset. He can't sit still, she thought. "I've got something serious to tell you," she said.

"You've done your work very well, don't worry," he answered, as he used up one paper towel after another.

"That's just what I wanted to talk to you about," Chris insisted. "I didn't come here to do work. I came because I thought our marriage was beginning to fall apart."

She feels the same way I do, he thought. But he continued with his cleaning.

"I've always respected your spiritual search, but I have mine, too," Chris said. "And I'm going to go on with it. I want you to understand that. I'm going to continue attending mass."

"I go to church, too."

"But what you're doing here is different, you know? You chose this way of communicating with God, and I've chosen a different one."

"I know that. I don't want to change."

"But meanwhile"—she took a deep breath, not knowing what his response would be—"meanwhile, something is happening to me. I want to speak to my angel, too."

She stood and went over to him. She began to gather the paper towels scattered on the ground.

"Do me a favor," she said, looking directly into her husband's eyes. "Don't leave me in the middle of the road."

THERE WAS A SMALL DINER NEXT TO THE gas station.

They sat near the window. It was early in the morning, and the world was still quiet. Outside was the desert, the immense, packed surface . . . and silence.

Chris missed Borrego Springs, Gringo Pass, and Indio. In those places, the desert had a face: mountains, valleys, stories of pioneers and conquistadors.

Here, though, the immense emptiness was all there was to see. And the sun. The sun that before long would color the world yellow, raise the temperature to 115 in the shade, and make life impossible.

The man behind the counter took their order. He was Chinese, and spoke with a strong accent—he could not have been here for very long. Chris imagined how many times the world had turned to bring the Chinese man to this luncheonette in the middle of the American desert.

They asked for coffee, bacon, and toast, and sat there in silence.

Chris looked at the man's eyes—they appeared to gaze to the horizon, the eyes of one whose soul had grown.

But no, he was not engaged in a holy exercise, or trying to develop his spiritual side. His was the gaze of boredom. He wasn't seeing anything—not the desert, not the road, and not even the two customers who had come in so early in the morning. He limited himself to the motions required—put the coffee in the coffeemaker, fry the eggs, say, "Can I help you?" or "Thank you." The meaning of his life appeared to have been left behind, or to have disappeared in the immensity of the treeless desert.

The coffee came. They began to sip it, in no hurry. They had nowhere to go.

Paulo looked at the car outside. It had done no good at all to have cleaned it two days before. It was covered with dust once again.

They heard a sound in the distance. In a few minutes, the first truck of the day would drive past. The man behind the counter might put his boredom and eggs and bacon aside, and go outside to try to find something, wanting to be a part of the world that was on the move, the world that passed by his diner. It was the only thing he could do; watch from a distance as the world went by. He probably no longer even dreamed of leaving the luncheonette behind and hitching a ride on one of the trucks to somewhere else. He was addicted to silence and emptiness.

The sound grew louder, but it didn't seem to be that of a truck engine. For a moment, Paulo's heart was filled with hope. But it was only a hope, nothing more. He tried not to think about it. The sound came closer and closer, and Chris turned to see what was happening outside.

Paulo stared at his coffee, afraid she might perceive his anxiety.

The windows of the restaurant rattled slightly with the noise. The counterman tried to ignore it—he knew the sound, and he didn't like it.

But Chris was fascinated. The horizon lit up with metallic reflections of the sun. The thundering engines seemed to shake the plants, the asphalt, the roof, and the windows of the restaurant.

With a roar, the Valkyries swept into the gas station. And the straight road, the flat desert, the tumbleweed, the Chinese man, and the two Brazilians in search of their angels, all felt their presence.

THE WOMEN, ON THEIR POWERFUL MOTOR-cycles, spun one way and then the other, dangerously close to one another, their machines shimmering in the hot air, their gloved hands toying skillfully with danger. They shouted out, as if to awaken the desert, to say they were alive and happy because it was morning.

Fear gripped Paulo's heart. Maybe they wouldn't stop there, maybe they were only trying to remind the counterman that life, joy, and skill still existed.

All at once, the rumbling stopped.

The Valkyries dismounted, shaking the desert from their bodies. They pounded the dust from their black leathers, and removed the colorful bandannas that they wore over their faces like bandits to keep the desert out of their lungs.

Then they entered the luncheonette.

Eight women.

They asked for nothing. The counterman seemed to know what they wanted—he was already placing eggs, bacon, and bread on the hot grill. Even with all the commotion, he continued to appear to be the obedient servant.

"Why is the radio turned off?" asked one of them.

The counterman turned it on.

"Louder!" said another.

Like a robot, he turned the radio to its loudest setting. The forgotten diner was suddenly transformed into a Manhattan disco. Some of the women kept time with the music by clapping their hands, while others carried on shouted conversations amidst the clamor.

But Chris, watching, saw that one of them moved not at all—the oldest of them, the one with long, curly red hair. She didn't enter into the conversation or the clapping of hands. She took no interest in the breakfast being prepared.

Intently, she stared at Paulo. And Paulo, resting his chin on his left hand, met the woman's gaze.

Chris felt a stab in her heart. *Why is he sitting like that?* Something very strange was happening. Perhaps the fact that she had been looking out at the horizon for so many days—or had been training so hard at the channeling—was changing the way she saw what went on around her. She had been having premonitions, and now they were manifesting.

She pretended not to notice that the two were eyeing each other. But her heart was giving her some inexplicable signals—and she couldn't tell whether they were good signals or bad.

Gene was right, Paulo thought. *It is easy to make contact with them.*

Slowly, the other Valkyries were beginning to perceive what was happening. First, they looked at the eldest, and then, following her gaze, turned to the table where Paulo and Chris were seated. Their conversation was silenced, and they no longer swayed in time to the music.

"Turn it off," the eldest said to the counterman.

As always, he obeyed. Now the only sound that could be heard was the sizzling of the eggs and bacon on the grill.

As her friends watched, the red-haired woman walked to the couple's table and simply stood there, looking at them. Then, without preamble, she spoke.

"Where did you get that ring?" she asked Paulo.

"At the same shop where you bought your brooch," he answered.

It was only then that Chris saw the metal brooch pinned to the leather jacket. It was made in the same design as the ring that Paulo wore on the ring finger of his left hand.

That's why he was resting his chin on his left hand.

She had already seen many rings in the Tradition of the Moon—of every color, metal and carved—always in the form of a serpent, the symbol of wisdom. But never had she seen one like the one her husband wore. J. had given Paulo that ring in 1982, when they were in Norway, saying that he was thereby completing "the Tradition of the Moon, a cycle that was interrupted by fear." And now, in the middle of the desert—a woman with a brooch of the same design.

"What do you want?" the redhead asked.

Paulo stood up, and the two stared at each other, face-to-face. Chris's heart was beating wildly—she was certain that it wasn't jealousy.

"What do you want?" she asked again.

"To speak with my angel. And something else."

She seized Paulo's hand and ran her fingers over his ring. Softening a bit, she seemed to become more feminine.

"If you bought that ring at the same place I did, you must know how it's made," she said, her eyes fixed on the serpents. "If not, then sell it to me. It's a beautiful piece."

It was simply a silver ring carved into two serpents. Each had two heads, and the design was quite simple.

Paulo said nothing.

"You don't know how to converse with angels, and this ring isn't yours," said the Valkyrie.

"I do know. Through channeling."

"Right," said the woman. "That's all that's required."

"I told you that there was something else I wanted."

"What is it?"

"Gene saw his angel. I want to see mine. I want to speak to my angel, face-to-face."

"Gene?" The woman's eyes searched the past, trying to recall who Gene was, where he lived.

"Yes, now I remember," she said. "He lives in the desert. Because that's where he met his angel."

"No. He is studying to become a master."

"This business of seeing your angel is just a myth. It's enough to converse with them."

Paulo stepped closer to the Valkyrie.

Chris knew the trick her husband was using: He called it "destabilization." Normally, two people converse at arm's length. When one of them approaches the other too closely, the other's thinking becomes disorganized.

"I want to see my angel." He was quite close to the woman, and he was staring at her.

"What for?" The Valkyrie appeared to be intimidated. The trick was working.

"Because I'm desperately in need of help. I have won important things for myself, but I am going to destroy them, because I tell myself that they have lost their meaning. I know it's not true. I know they are still important, and that if I destroy them, I'll be destroying myself, as well."

He maintained a neutral tone of voice, showing no emotion.

"When I learned that channeling was all that was needed in order to speak with my angel, I lost interest. It was no longer a challenge, but rather something I knew very well. I realized that my path to magic was about to end; the unknown was becoming too familiar to me."

Chris was shocked: Why was he making this confession in such a public place, in front of people whom he had never seen before?

"In order to continue along my path, I need something more," he finished. "I need mountains that are taller and taller."

The Valkyrie said nothing for a moment.

"If I teach you how to see your angel," she said, "your desire to seek out taller and taller mountains may disappear. And that's not always a good thing."

"No, that will never disappear," Paulo replied. "What will vanish is the idea that the mountains I've conquered are too small. I will be able to keep alive my love for what I've accomplished. That's what my master was trying to say to me."

Maybe he's talking about our marriage, too, Chris thought.

The Valkyrie held out her hand to Paulo.

"My name is M.," she said.

"My name is S.," Paulo answered.

Chris was startled. Paulo had given his magic name! Very few people knew that secret, since the only way to cause a certain kind of evil to a magus is by using his magic name. Only those who were completely trustworthy were allowed to know the name.

Paulo had just met this woman. He couldn't trust her that much.

"But you can call me Valhalla," the red-haired woman continued.

That's the name of the Vikings' paradise, Paulo thought, and he told her his given name in return.

The redhead appeared to relax a bit. For the first time, she looked at Chris, seated at the table.

"In order to see an angel, three things are needed," said the Valkyrie, turning back to Paulo as if Chris didn't exist. "And, in addition to those three things, courage is needed. A woman's courage, not a man's."

Paulo made it appear that he was paying no attention.

"Tomorrow, we will be near Tucson," Valhalla said. "Come to see us at noon, if your ring is authentic."

Paulo got the map out of the car, and Valhalla showed him the place where they should meet. One of the other Valkyries told Valhalla that her breakfast was getting cold. She turned back to her place at the counter and asked the man to turn on the radio again.

For a long time, Paulo and Chris sat over their coffee, watching the Valkyries eat.

Finally, the women got up and began to leave. As Valhalla reached the door, Paulo called out, "What are the three conditions for conversing with one's angel?"

Quietly, the redhead replied: "Break a pact. Accept forgiveness. And make a bet."

Paulo and Chris looked out at the city below. For the first time in almost three weeks, they were in a real hotel—room service, bar, and breakfast in bed.

It was six in the evening, the hour in which they had gotten into the habit of practicing their channeling exercises. But Paulo was fast asleep.

Chris knew that the meeting that morning at the diner had changed everything; if she wanted to talk to her angel, she would have to do it on her own.

They had spoken little during the trip to Tucson. She had asked him only why he had divulged his magic name. Paulo answered that Valhalla had given him hers, and he could do no less.

Perhaps he was telling the truth, perhaps this was what he believed, but Chris wondered. She was a woman, and she saw things that men don't. She thought that Paulo might want to talk to her later that night.

Chris called the desk clerk and asked where the nearest bookstore was located. There was none nearby, he said; she would have to drive. She thought about it for a few moments, and then got the car keys. They were in a big city; if Paulo awoke, he would think that she had gone exploring.

She became lost in the traffic several times, but eventually found a huge shopping mall. One of the shops made keys, and she had a copy made of the keys to the car.

She wanted to have one, just to be secure.

In a bookstore, she leafed through a volume until she found what she was looking for:

VALKYRIES: the nymphs at Wotan's palace.

She had no idea who Wotan was, but that wasn't important.

Messengers of the gods, they led heroes to their death—and then to paradise.

Messengers. *Like the angels,* she thought. Death and paradise. Also like the angels.

They excite combatants with the love that their charm excites in their hearts, and through the example of bravery at the battlefront, mounted on steeds as fast as the clouds and as deafening as a thunderstorm.

They couldn't have chosen a better name, she thought.

At the same time, they symbolize both the inebriation of courage and rest for the warrior, the adventure of love in battle, encounter, and loss.

Right, absolutely. Paulo would want to talk to her.

THEY WENT DOWN TO HAVE DINNER AT their own hotel—even though Paulo had tried to insist that they walk a bit, get to know this large city built in the middle of the desert. But Chris said she was tired, wanted to get to bed early, enjoy the comforts.

They made small talk throughout the meal. Paulo was exaggeratedly attentive. Chris knew that her husband was waiting for the right moment. So she made it appear that she was interested in everything he said, and showed enthusiasm when he said that Tucson had the most complete desert museum in the world.

In his enthusiasm, he mentioned that the museum included live coyotes, snakes, and scorpions, with a great deal of information concerning them. They could spend the entire day there.

She said she'd like very much to see it.

"You could go tomorrow morning," Paulo said.

"But Valhalla mentioned noontime."

"You don't have to be there."

"It's a strange hour," she answered. "No one spends much time in the desert at high noon. We learned that—in the worst way possible."

Paulo had thought it strange, too. But he didn't want to miss the chance; he was afraid Valhalla might change her mind, despite the ring and everything else.

He changed the subject, and Chris could sense her husband's anxiety. They went back to small talk for a time. They drank an entire bottle of wine, and she was sleepy. Paulo suggested they go right up.

"I don't know if you should go tomorrow," he said.

She had already tasted of everything—the meal, the place, Paulo's anxiety. She was enjoying the chance of confirming for herself that she really knew this man well. But now it was getting late, and it was time to give him a definite answer.

"I'm going with you. No matter what."

He was irritated. He told her that she was jealous, and that she was spoiling his process.

"Jealous of whom?"

"Of the Valkyries. Of Valhalla."

"That's crazy."

"But this is *my* quest. I brought you with me because I wanted you at my side. But there are certain things I have to do alone."

"I want to go with you," she said.

"Magic has never been important to you before. Why now?"

"Because I began the journey. And I've asked that I not be abandoned in the middle of the road," she answered, putting the matter to rest.

❀

The silence was complete.

Everyone was wearing sunglasses against the blinding sun. Everyone—except Chris and Valhalla. Chris had removed hers so that Valhalla would know that she was looking directly into her eyes.

Chris had been bearing up under the woman's gaze for some time.

The minutes passed, and no one spoke. The only word that had been spoken the entire time had been Paulo's hello when they had arrived at the meeting place. His greeting had not been returned. Valhalla simply approached Chris and stood directly before her.

And, since that moment, nothing else had happened.

We must have been doing this for twenty minutes, Chris thought, but she didn't know how much time had actually elapsed. The glare of the sun, the heat, and the silence confused her.

She tried to distract herself a bit. They were at

the foot of a mountain—wonderful, the desert once again contained mountains! Behind Valhalla, an entrance had been carved into the stone. Chris tried to imagine what the door led to, and found that she wasn't able to think clearly—just as on the day they had returned from the salt lake.

No one was perspiring—the dryness of the air was so great that all moisture evaporated immediately, as Gene had said. Chris knew that they were rapidly dehydrating—even though she had drunk as much water as possible, and even though she had prepared for the noonday desert. And even though she wasn't nude.

The other Valkyries had formed a semicircle; they wore their kerchiefs on their heads, in the manner of gypsies or pirates. Valhalla alone was bareheaded—her kerchief encircled her neck. The sun seemed not to bother her.

She is dismissing me with her eyes, Chris thought.

She knew this could not continue forever. There was a limit. She didn't know what that limit was, nor how or when she would know, but very soon, the sun would begin to be damaging. Meanwhile, everyone continued immobile—and all of this had happened because of her. Because she had insisted on coming along. *Messengers of the gods, they lead the heroes to death and to paradise.*

She had made a bad mistake, but now it was too late. She had come because her angel had required that she do so; her angel had said that Paulo was going to need her that afternoon.

No, no, it wasn't a mistake. My angel insisted that I be here, she thought.

Her angel—she was conversing with her angel! Nobody knew it, not even Paulo.

She began to feel dizzy, and she was certain she would faint soon. But she was going to see it through—it was no longer just a matter of being at her husband's side, or obeying her angel, or being jealous. Now it was a woman's pride—face-to-face with another woman.

"Put your glasses on," Valhalla said. "This sun could blind you."

"You're not wearing glasses," she answered. "And you're not afraid."

Valhalla gave a signal, and suddenly, the blazing light of the sun was multiplied a dozen times.

The Valkyries were using the mirrors on their motorcycles to reflect the sun directly into Chris's eyes. She saw a gleaming semicircle, knitted her brows, and kept her gaze upon Valhalla.

But she could no longer see clearly. The woman's image appeared to grow and grow, and the confusion in her mind increased. She felt she was about to fall, and at that moment, leather-covered arms came to her support.

PAULO WATCHED VALHALLA CATCH CHRIS in her arms. All of this could have been avoided. He could have insisted that she remain at the hotel—no matter what she was thinking. From the moment that he had first seen the brooch, he had known which tradition the Valkyries came from.

They had also seen his ring, and they knew that he had been tested in many ways. That it would be difficult to frighten him. But they would do everything possible to test the fiber of any stranger who entered their group. Even if that stranger was his wife.

But they could not prevent Chris, nor anyone else, from learning what they wanted to learn. They had taken a vow: Everything that was hidden had to be revealed. Chris was now being tested in the first great virtue of those who seek the spiritual path: courage.

The Valkyrie looked at Paulo. "Help me."

Paulo helped her support his wife. They took her to the car and laid her down on the backseat.

"Don't worry. She'll come around very quickly. With a serious headache."

He wasn't worried. He was proud.

Valhalla went to her cycle and brought a canteen. Paulo noted that she had already donned her sunglasses—she must have reached her limit, as well.

She bathed Chris's forehead in water, and dabbed some on her wrists and behind her ears. She opened her eyes, blinked several times, and sat up.

"Break a pact," she said, looking at the Valkyrie.

"You are an interesting woman," Valhalla said, passing her hand across Chris's face. "Put your glasses on."

Valhalla caressed Chris's hair. And even though both were now wearing dark glasses, Paulo knew they were staring at each other.

THEY WALKED TO THE STRANGE DOOR IN the mountain.

Valhalla turned to the other Valkyries. "For love. For victory. And for the glory of God."

The same phrase J. had used. The words of those who know angels.

The Valkyries started their engines, blowing up a cloud of dust. The women did the same maneuvers they had at the gas station—passing closely by each other—and, minutes later, they had disappeared around the mountain.

Valhalla turned to Chris and Paulo.

"Let's go in," she said.

There was no door, just a grate. On it hung a sign:

DANGER

THE FEDERAL GOVERNMENT

PROHIBITS ENTRY

VIOLATORS WILL BE PROSECUTED

"Don't believe it," said the Valkyrie. "They're not going to spend any time guarding this."

It was an old, abandoned gold mine. Valhalla, carrying a lantern, began to move forward carefully, so as not to bump her head on the passage beams. Paulo noticed that here and there the floor had collapsed. It might have been dangerous, but now wasn't the time to think about it.

As they went deeper, the temperature fell, and it even became pleasant. He was worried about a lack of air, but Valhalla was moving along as if she knew the place well—she must have been there many times, and she was still alive. Now wasn't the time to think about that, either.

After walking for ten minutes or so, the Valkyrie halted. They sat on the floor of the passage, and she placed the lantern in the middle of their circle.

"Angels," she said. "Angels are visible to those who accept the light. And break the pact with the darkness."

"I have no pact with the darkness," Paulo responded. "I had one. But no longer."

"I'm not talking about a pact with Lucifer, or with Satan, or with . . ." She began to speak the names of various demons, and her face looked strange.

"Don't say those names," Paulo interrupted. "God is in the words, and the devil as well."

Valhalla laughed. "It looks as if you've learned the lesson. Now, break the pact."

"I have no pact with evil," Paulo repeated.

"I'm talking about your pact with defeat."

Paulo thought of what J. had said—about destroying what we love most. But J. had said nothing about pacts; he knew Paulo well enough to know that his pact with evil had been broken a long time ago. The silence within the mine was worse than in the desert. Not a sound was heard, except Valhalla's voice—which sounded different.

"We have a contract, you and I: not to win when victory is possible," she insisted.

"I have never made any such pact," Paulo said for the third time.

"Everyone has. At some point in our lives, we all enter into such an agreement. That's why there is an angel with a burning sword at the gates to paradise. To allow entry only to those who have broken that pact."

Yes, she's right, thought Chris. *Everyone has made this pact.*

"Do you find me attractive?" Valhalla asked, once again changing the tone of her voice.

"You are a beautiful woman," Paulo answered.

"One day, when I was still an adolescent, I saw my best friend crying. We were inseparable, and we loved each other completely, and I asked what had happened. When I insisted on knowing, she told me that her boyfriend was in love with me. I didn't know that, and that day I made the pact. Without really knowing why, I began to gain weight, to take poor care of myself, to become unattractive. Because—unconsciously—I felt that my beauty was a curse, and had caused suffering for my best friend.

"Before long, I had destroyed all meaning in my life because I just didn't care about myself anymore. I reached the point that everything about my life became unbearable: I thought about dying."

Valhalla laughed.

"As you can see, I broke the pact."

"True," Paulo said.

"Yes, it is true," Chris said. "You are lovely."

"We are in the heart of the mountain," the Valkyrie continued. "Outside, the sun is shining, and here there is only darkness. But the temperature is pleasant, we can sleep, we have nothing to worry about. This is the darkness of the pact."

She raised her hand to the zipper of her leather jacket.

"Break the pact," she said. "For the glory of God. For love. And for victory."

She began to lower the zipper slowly. She wore nothing beneath the jacket.

The light from the lantern caused a medallion between her breasts to gleam.

"Take it," she said.

Paulo touched the medallion. The archangel Michael.

"Take it from around my neck."

He removed the medallion and held it in his hands.

"Both of you, hold the medallion."

Suddenly, Chris blurted out, "I don't need to see my angel! I don't need to. Just speaking will do."

Paulo held the medallion in his hand.

"I've already begun talking with my angel," Chris went on, more quietly. "I know that I can, and that's good enough."

Paulo didn't believe her. But Valhalla knew that it was the truth. She had read it in her eyes when they were outside. She also knew that her angel wanted her to be there with her husband.

Nevertheless, she had to test her courage. It was the rule of the Tradition.

"All right," the Valkyrie said. With a rapid movement, she blew out the lantern. The darkness was total.

"Put the cord around your neck," she said to Paulo. "And hold the medallion with both hands joined, in prayer."

Paulo did as he was told. He was fearful of a darkness so complete, and he was remembering things he would rather not think about.

He felt Valhalla approaching him from behind. Her hands touched his head.

The darkness seemed almost solid. Nothing, not a scintilla of light, entered there.

Valhalla began to pray in a strange language. At first, he tried to identify the words she was saying. Then, as her fingers moved across his head, Paulo felt the medallion growing hot. He concentrated on the heat in his hands.

The darkness was changing. Various scenes from his life began to pass before him. Light and shadow, light and shadow, and—suddenly, he was once again in darkness.

"I don't want to remember that . . ." he pleaded with the Valkyrie.

"Remember! Whatever it is, try to remember every minute of it."

The darkness brought terror to him, the terror he had experienced fourteen years earlier.

❁

When he woke up, he found a note on the coffee table: "I love you. I'll be right back." At the bottom, she had written the date: "25 May 1974."

Funny. To put the date on a love note.

He had awakened a bit dizzy, still startled by the dream. In it, the director of the recording studio was offering him a job. He didn't need a job: The director actually functioned more like his employee—his and his partner's. Their records were at the top of the charts, selling thousands of copies, and letters were arriving from all corners of Brazil, from people wanting to know what the Alternative Society was.

All you have to do is listen to the words of the song, *he thought to himself. It wasn't really a song—it was a mantra from a magic ritual, with the words of the Beast of the Apocalypse being read in the background in a low voice. Whoever sang the song would be invoking the forces of darkness. And everyone was singing it.*

He and his partner had done the whole thing. The royalties they earned were being used to buy a lot near Rio de Janeiro. There they would recreate what, almost one hundred years earlier, the Beast had tried to establish in Cefalu, Sicily. But the Beast was expelled by the Italian authorities. The Beast had erred on many points—he had not gathered a sufficient number of disciples, and he did not know how to earn money. The Beast told everyone that his number was 666, and that he had come to create a world where the strong would be served by the weak, and the only law was that everyone do as they desired. But the Beast didn't know how to spread the ideas—few people had taken the Beast's words seriously.

He and his partner, Raul Seixas, well, they were completely different! Raul sang, and the entire country listened. They were young, and they were earning money. Yes, it was true that Brazil was in the hands of a military dictatorship, but the government was concerned about guerrillas. They couldn't waste their time with a rock singer. Just the opposite: The authorities felt that rock music kept the country's youth away from communism.

He drank his coffee standing at the window. He was going to take a walk, and meet later with his partner. It didn't bother him at all that nobody knew who he was, while his friend was famous. What mattered was that they were earning money, and this would allow them to put their ideas into practice. People from the world of music, and the world of magic—ah, they knew! His anonymity with regard to the general public was even rather funny—more than once, he had had the pleasure of hearing someone comment on his work—without knowing that the author was listening nearby.

He donned his sneakers. As he was tying the laces, he felt dizzy.

He raised his head. The apartment seemed darker than it should have been. The sun was shining outside, and he had just left the window. Something was burning—an electrical appliance, maybe, because the stove was disconnected. He looked throughout the apartment. Nothing.

The air was heavy. He decided to go out right away—without tying his sneakers, he started to leave, but realized that he really wasn't feeling well.

Could be something I ate, he said to himself. But when he ate something that was off, his entire body usually gave him a signal, and he knew that. He wasn't nauseated, didn't feel like vomiting. Just a kind of dizziness that didn't seem to want to pass.

Dark. The darkness grew; it seemed like a gray cloud around him. He felt the dizziness again. Yes, it had to be something he had eaten—Or maybe an acid flashback, he thought. But he hadn't tried LSD in five years. The delayed effects had disappeared after the first six months, and never returned.

He was frightened, he had to get out.

He opened the door—the dizziness was coming and going, and he might get worse out in the street. Better to stay home and wait. The note was there on the table—she would be home shortly—he could wait. They could go together to the pharmacy or to a doctor, although he hated doctors. It couldn't be anything serious. No one has a heart attack at age twenty-six.

No one.

He sat down on the couch. He needed some distraction. He shouldn't think about her, or the time would pass even more slowly. He tried to read the paper, but the dizziness, the lightheadedness, came and went, stronger each time. Something was pulling him into a black hole that appeared to have formed in the middle of the room. He began to hear noises—laughing, voices, things breaking. That had never happened—never! Whenever he had taken anything, he knew he was drugged, knew it was a hallucination and would pass with time. But this—this was terribly real!

No, no, it couldn't be real. The reality was the rugs, the curtains, the bookshelves, the coffee table with the leftovers of bread on it. He made an effort to concentrate on the scene surrounding him, but the feeling of a black hole in front of him, the voices, the laughter, all continued.

None of this was happening. Definitely! He had practiced magic for six years. Performed all the rituals. He knew it was nothing more than suggestion. A psychological effect that was playing on his imagination. Nothing more.

His panic was increasing, and the dizziness was more pronounced—pulling to the outside of his body, toward a dark world, toward that laughter, those voices, those noises—real!

I cannot let myself be afraid. Fear will make it come back. *He tried to control himself, went to the sink and bathed his face. He felt a bit better, the feeling seemed to have passed. He put his sneakers on and tried to forget about it. He toyed with the idea of telling his partner he had entered into a trance, had been in contact with demons.*

But he had only to think about that, and the dizziness returned—more strongly.

"I'll be right back," the note said, and she hadn't come!

I never achieved concrete results in the astral plane, *he thought. He had never seen anything. No angels, no devils, no spirits of the dead. The Beast wrote in his diary that he was able to make things materialize, but he was lying, the Beast had never gotten that far. He knew that. The Beast had failed. He liked the Beast's ideas because they were rebellious, chic. And very few people had ever heard them. And people are always more respectful of those who speak of things no one understands. As for the rest—Hare Krishna, Children of God, the Church of Satan, Maharishi—everyone knew about those. The Beast—the Beast was just for the chosen few! "The law of the powerful," one of his books talked about.*

The Beast was on the cover of Sgt. Pepper's Lonely Hearts Club Band, *one of the Beatles's best known records—and almost no one knew it. Maybe not even the Beatles knew what they were doing when they placed that photograph there.*

The phone rang. It might be his girlfriend. But if she had written, "I'll be right back," why would she be phoning?

Only if something was happening.

That's why she hadn't come. The intervals between bouts of dizziness were growing shorter and shorter, and everything was turning black again. He knew—something was telling him—that he couldn't let that feeling take him over. Something terrible might happen—he might enter into that darkness and never return. He had to maintain control at any cost—he needed to occupy his mind, or that thing would dominate him.

The phone. He concentrated on the phone. Speak, converse, think of other things, take his mind off that darkness, the phone was a miracle, a solution. He knew it. He knew that somehow he couldn't surrender. He had to answer the phone.

"Hello?"

It was a woman's voice. But it wasn't his girlfriend— it was Argelia.

"Paulo?"

He didn't answer.

"Paulo, can you hear me? I need you to come over to my house! Something strange is going on!"

"What's happening?"

"You know, Paulo! Explain it to me, for God's sake!"

He hung up before he heard something he didn't want to hear. It wasn't a delayed drug effect. It wasn't a symptom of insanity. It wasn't a heart attack. It was real. Argelia had participated in the rituals, and "that" was happening to her, too.

He panicked. He sat there without thinking for a few minutes, and the darkness began to take him over, coming closer and closer, causing him to step to the edge of the lake of death.

He was going to die—for everything he had done without believing, for the many people he had involved without knowing it, for so much evil spread about in the name of what was good. He would die, and the Darkness would go on, because it was manifesting itself now, before his very eyes, demonstrating that things really worked, collecting what was owed for the time in which it had been used, and he had to pay—because he didn't want to know what the price was before, thought it was for free, that everything was a lie or just suggestion!

His years in the Jesuit school came back to him, and he prayed for the strength needed to get back to a church, ask forgiveness, pray that at least God would save his soul. He had to be able to do it. He found that as long as he could keep his mind busy, he was able to dominate the dizziness, at least partly. He needed time to get to the church . . . What a ridiculous idea!

He looked at the bookcase, and resolved that he would calculate how many records he owned—after all, he had always put that task off! Yes, it was important to know the exact number of records, and he began to count: one, two, three . . . he did it! He was able to overcome the dizziness, the black hole that was pulling him in. He counted all of the records—and then counted them again, to make certain he was correct. Now the books. He had to count in order to know how many books he had. Did he have more books than records? He began to count. The dizziness halted, and he had so many books. And magazines. And alternative newspapers. He would count everything, write it down, really know how many things he owned. It was so important.

He was counting the silverware when he heard the key turn in the lock. She was here, finally. But he couldn't allow himself to be distracted—he couldn't even talk about what was happening; any moment now, it was all going to stop. He was certain of it.

She went straight to the kitchen, and hugged him, crying.

"Help me! Something strange is happening. You know what it is, help me!"

He didn't want to lose his count of the silverware—that was his salvation. Keep the mind busy. Better if she hadn't arrived—it didn't help. And she thought the same as Argelia—that he knew everything, that he knew how to stop it.

"Keep your mind busy!" he shouted, as if he were possessed. "Count how many records you have! And how many books!"

She looked at him without understanding what he was talking about. Like a robot, she walked to the bookcase.

But she didn't get there. She suddenly threw herself to the floor.

"I want my mother . . ." she said, over and over. "I want my mother . . . "

He did too. He wanted to phone his parents, ask for help—his parents whom he never saw, who belonged to a middle-class world he had abandoned long ago. He tried to go on with the silverware count, but she was there, crying like a child, pulling at her hair.

That was too much. He was responsible for what was happening, because he loved her, and had taught her the rituals, guaranteed that she could get what she wanted, that things were improving day by day (although he never for a moment believed what he was saying!). Now she was there, begging for help, trusting in him—and he had no idea what to do.

For a moment, he thought of issuing an order, but he had already lost his silverware count, and the black hole came back suddenly with even greater strength.

"You help me," he said. "I don't know what to do."

And he began to cry.

He was crying out of fear, as when he was a child. He wanted his parents, as she did. He was bathed in a cold sweat, and was certain he would die. He seized her hand, and her hands were cold, too, even though her clothing was soaked in perspiration. He went to the bathroom to wash his face—as he used to do when the effects of the drugs were really strong. Maybe it would work with regard to "that," too. The hallway seemed immense, the thing was stronger now—he was no longer counting records, books, pencils, silverware. There was no place to hide.

"Running water."

The thought came from some far corner of his mind, some place that the darkness had not seemed to penetrate. Running water! Yes, there was a power in darkness, in delirium, in madness—but there were other things!

"Running water," he said to her, as he bathed his face. "Running water keeps the evil away."

She heard the certainty in his voice. He knew, he knew everything. He would save her.

He turned the shower on, and they both huddled under it—with their clothing, their documents, their money. The cold water moistened their bodies, and, for the first time since he had awakened, he experienced a sense of relief. The dizziness vanished. They stayed for two or three hours under the spray, without speaking, shivering from fear and the cold. They stepped out only once, to phone Argelia and tell her to do the same thing. The dizziness returned, and they had to flee back into the shower. There, everything seemed calm, but they needed desperately to understand what was happening.

"I never believed it," he said.

She looked at him, not understanding. Two years earlier, they had been two hippies, without a cent to their name, and now his songs were being heard all over the country. He was at the peak of success—even though few people knew his name; and he had been saying that it was all the result of the rituals, the occult studies, the power of magic.

"I never believed it," he continued. "Or I never would have walked those paths! I never would have risked myself, or you."

"Do something, for the love of God!" she said. "We can't stay here in the shower forever!"

He left the shower again, checking whether the dizziness and the black hole were still there. He went to the bookcase and came back with the Bible. He had a Bible in the house only so that he could read from the Revelation to John, be certain about the reign of the Beast. He had done everything as called for by the Beast's followers—and, in his heart, he had believed none of it.

"Let's pray to God," he said. He felt ridiculous, demoralized before this woman whom he had tried to impress for all those years. He was weak, he was going to die. He had to humiliate himself, beg for forgiveness. What was most important now was the saving of his soul. In the end, everything was true.

He embraced the Bible, and recited prayers he had learned as a child—Our Father, Hail Mary, the Creed. She refused at the beginning, and then recited them with him.

Then he opened the book at random. The water poured down on the pages, but he was able to read the story of someone who had asked something of Jesus, and Jesus said that he must maintain the faith. The man answered: "Lord, I believe—help me in my incredulity."

"Lord, I believe, help me in my incredulity!" he shouted through the sound of the falling water.

"Lord, I believe, help me in my incredulity!" he said in a whisper, through his sobs.

He began to feel strangely calm. If the terrible evil they had experienced really existed, then it was true that the kingdom of heaven did, as well, and along with it, everything else that he had learned and then denied throughout his life.

"The eternal life exists," he said, knowing that he would never again believe in those words. "I don't care if I die. You cannot fear death, either."

"I'm not afraid," she answered. "I'm not afraid, but I think it's unfair. It's a pity."

They were only twenty-six. It really was a pity.

"We have been through everything someone our age could have experienced," he answered. "Most people haven't even come close."

"That's true," she said. "We can die."

He lifted his face, and the sound of the water in his ears seemed like thunder. He was no longer crying, nor afraid; he was only paying the price for his insolence.

"Lord, I believe, help me in my incredulity," he repeated. "We want to make an exchange. We offer you anything, absolutely anything, in return for the salvation of our souls. We offer our lives, or everything we own. Please accept, my lord."

She looked at him with contempt. The man she had admired so. The powerful, mysterious, courageous man she had so admired, who had convinced so many people with regard to the Alternative Society, who had preached about a world where anything was allowed, where the strong ruled over the weak. That man was there, crying, screaming for his mother, praying like a child, and saying that he had always been courageous—because he had believed in nothing.

He turned, and said they should both look up and make the exchange. She did so. She had lost her man, her faith, and her hope. She had nothing else to lose.

He placed his hand on the faucet, and slowly shut it down. Now they could die; God had forgiven them.

The stream of water turned to droplets, and then there was complete silence. Soaked to the bone, they looked at each other. The dizziness, the black hole, the laughter, and the noises, all had disappeared.

HE WAS LYING IN A WOMAN'S LAP, CRYING. Her hand was caressing his head.

"I made that pact," he said tearfully.

"No," the woman answered. "It was a trade."

Paulo clutched the archangel medallion. Yes, there had been a trade—and the punishment was severe. Two days after that morning in 1974, they were imprisoned by the Brazilian political police and accused of subversion based on the Alternative Society. He was placed in a dark cell, similar to the black hole he had seen in his living room. He was threatened with death, and he gave in, but it was a trade. When he was released, he split up with his partner and was expelled from the world of music for a long time. No one would give him a job. But it was a trade.

Other members of the group had not made the trade. They survived in the "black hole," and regarded him as a coward. He lost his friends, his security, his desire to go on living. For years, he was afraid to go out into the street—the dizziness might return, the police could appear again. And, even worse, after his release from prison he never saw his girlfriend again. At times, he regretted the trade—it would have been better to have died than to have to live that way. But now it was too late to go back.

"There was a pact," Valhalla said. "What was it?"

"I promised I would abandon my dreams."

For seven years, he paid the price for the trade. But God was generous, and allowed him to rebuild his life. The director of the recording studio, the same person he had dreamed about that May morning, gave him a job and became his only friend. He went back to composing, but every time his work brought some success, something wound up happening, and everything went down the drain.

He remembered J's words: People destroy what they love.

"I always figured it was part of the bargain," he said.

"No," Valhalla said. "God was severe, but you were more severe than he was."

"I promised that I would never grow again. I thought that I could no longer trust myself."

The Valkyrie held his head to her bare breasts.

"Tell me about the dread," she said. "The dread that I saw when we met at the luncheonette."

"The terror . . ." He didn't know how to begin, because he felt he would sound absurd. "The terror doesn't allow me to sleep at night, or rest during the day."

Now Chris understood her angel. She had to be here, hearing this, because he would never have told her . . .

". . . and now I have a wife that I love, I found J., I walked the holy Road to Santiago, I've written books. I'm being faithful to my dreams again, and that's where the dread comes from. Because everything is going the way I would like it to, and I know that soon it will all be destroyed." It was terrible to say that. He had never said it to anyone—not even himself. He knew that Chris was there, hearing it all. And he was ashamed.

"That's the way it was with the songs," he said, forcing himself to go on. "That's the way it's been with everything I've done since then. Nothing has lasted more than two years."

He felt Valhalla's hands removing the medallion from around his neck. He stood. He didn't want her to light the lantern, because he lacked the courage to confront Chris.

But Valhalla lit the lantern, and the three made their way out in silence.

"We two are going out first, and you come along later," Valhalla said to Paulo as they were reaching the end of the tunnel.

Paulo was certain that, just as with his girlfriend

of fourteen years earlier, Chris would never again trust him.

"Today, I believe in what I'm doing," he tried to say before the other two left. It sounded like a plea for forgiveness, like self-justification.

No one answered. After a few more steps, Valhalla extinguished the lantern. There was now sufficient light for them to see.

"From the moment that you set foot outside," the Valkyrie said, "promise, in the name of the archangel Michael, that never again—*never again*—will you raise your hand against yourself."

"I'm afraid to say that," he answered. "Because I don't know how to comply."

"You have no choice, if you want to see your angel."

"I didn't realize what I was doing to myself. I might continue with the same kind of self-betrayal."

"Now you know," Valhalla said. "And the truth gives you freedom."

Paulo nodded his head.

"You will still have many problems in your life, some of them normal, some of them difficult. But, from now on, only God's hand will be responsible for everything—you will interfere no more."

"I promise in the name of Saint Michael."

The women went out. He waited a moment, and then began to walk. He had been in the darkness long enough.

THE RAYS OF LIGHT, REFLECTING FROM the stone walls, showed the way. There was the grated door, a door leading to a prohibited kingdom. A door that frightened him. Because out there was the kingdom of light, and he had been living for years in the darkness. A door that appeared to be closed—but, for anyone who approached it, it was open.

The door to the light was there in front of him. He wanted to pass through. He could see the golden light of the sun outside, but he decided not to put on his sunglasses. He needed the light. And he knew that the archangel Michael was at his side, sweeping away the darkness with his lance.

For years he had believed in the implacable hand of God, in his punishment. But it was his own hand, not God's, that had wrought such destruction. Never, for the rest of his life, would he do that again.

"Break the pact," he said to the darkness of the mine and to the desert light. "God has the right to destroy me. I do not."

He thought of the books he had written, and was happy. The year would end without any problem—because the pact had been broken. There was no doubt that problems would arise in his work, in love, and along the path to magic—serious problems or passing problems, as Valhalla had said. But from now on, he would battle side by side with his guardian angel.

You must have made a tremendous effort, he said to his angel. *And, in the end, I spoiled everything, and you couldn't understand it.*

His angel was listening. The angel knew about the pact, too, and was happy at not having to devote efforts to keeping Paulo from destroying himself.

Paulo found the door and passed through it. The sun blinded him for a moment, but he kept his eyes open—he needed the light. He saw the figures of Valhalla and Chris approaching. "Put your hand on his shoulder," Valhalla said to Chris. "Be a witness."

Chris obeyed.

Valhalla took a few drops of water from her canteen and made a cross on his forehead—as if baptizing him. Then she knelt, and told them to kneel as well.

"In the name of the archangel Michael, the pact was known in heaven. In the name of the archangel Michael, the pact was broken."

She placed the medallion on his forehead, and asked that he repeat her words:

Sainted angel of the Lord,
My zealous guardian . . .

The prayer from childhood echoed from the walls of the mountain, and spread throughout that part of the desert.

If I trust in you,
The divine piety
Will rule me always, and guard,
Govern, and enlighten.
Amen.

"Amen," said Chris.
"Amen," he repeated.

PEOPLE WERE APPROACHING THEM CURIOUSLY.

"They're lesbians," said one.

"They're crazy," said another.

The Valkyries paid no attention, but continued with what they were doing. They had tied one kerchief to another, forming a kind of rope. They sat on the ground in a circle—their arms resting on their knees, holding the joined kerchiefs.

Valhalla was in the middle, on foot. People continued to arrive. When a small multitude had formed, the Valkyries began to chant a psalm.

By the rivers of Babylon,
There we sat down, yea, and wept.
We hung our harps upon the willows
In the midst of it.

The people watched, understanding none of it. It was not the first time these women had appeared in the city. They had been there before, speaking of strange things—although certain words were similar to those uttered by television preachers.

"Have courage." Valhalla's voice rang out clearly and strongly. "Open your heart, and listen to what your dreams tell you. Follow those dreams, because only a person who is not ashamed can manifest the glory of God."

"The desert's made them crazy," a woman said.

Some people left immediately. They were fed up with preaching.

"There is no sin but the lack of love," Valhalla continued. "Have courage, be capable of loving, even if love appears to be a treacherous and terrible thing. Be happy in love. Be joyful in victory. Follow the dictates of your heart."

"That's impossible," someone in the crowd said. "People have obligations."

Valhalla turned in the direction of the voice. She was doing it—people were paying attention! Different from five years earlier, when no one came near them during their appearances in the city.

"We have children. We have husbands and wives. People have to earn a living," another person said.

"Well, meet your obligations. But obligations never prevented anyone from following their dreams. Remember that you are a manifestation of the absolute, and do only those things in your lives that are *worth the effort*. Only those who do that will understand the great transformations that are yet to be seen."

The Conspiracy, Chris thought, as she listened. She remembered the time long ago when she had sung in the plaza with others from her church, to save people from sin. In those days, no one spoke of a New Age—they spoke of the coming of Christ, of punishment and hell. There was no Conspiracy, such as now.

She walked through the crowd and found Paulo. He was sitting on a bench, far from the gathering.

"How long are we going to travel with them?" she asked.

"Until Valhalla teaches me how to see angels."

"But we've been here for almost a month."

"She cannot refuse me. She swore on the Tradition. She has to keep her vow."

The crowd was growing in size. Chris was thinking how difficult it must be to talk to the people gathered there.

"They're not going to take the Valkyries seriously," she said. "Not with the way they're dressed, and with those motorcycles."

"They have been fighting for some very old ideas,". Paulo said. "Nowadays, soldiers dress in camouflage. They disguise themselves, and they hide. But the old warriors dressed in colorful outfits, much more obvious on the field of battle.

"They wanted the enemy to see them. They took pride in battle."

"Why are they doing this? Why preach in public parks and in bars and in the middle of the desert? Why are they helping us to speak to our angels?"

He lit a cigarette. "You joke about a Conspiracy, but you're right," he said. "There is a Conspiracy."

She laughed. No, no, there was no Conspiracy. She had used that term because her husband's friends acted like secret agents, always careful not to discuss certain things when others were present, always changing the subject—although they had sworn, all of them had, that there was nothing occult in the Tradition.

But Paulo seemed to be serious.

"The gates to Paradise have been reopened," he said. "God banished the angel with the burning sword who was at the gate. For some time—no one is certain for how long—anyone could enter, since it was obvious that the gates were open."

As he was speaking to Chris, Paulo recalled the abandoned gold mine. Up until that day—a week ago—he had chosen to remain outside of paradise.

"What guarantees entry?"

"Faith. And the Tradition," he answered.

They walked over to an ice cream wagon and bought cones. Valhalla continued to speak, and her sermon appeared to be endless. Before long, she might even try to get the spectators to participate, at which point it would probably end.

"Does everyone know that the gates are open?" Chris asked.

"Some people have noticed—and they are calling the others. But there's a problem."

Paulo pointed to a monument in the middle of the square. "Let's suppose that paradise is there. And every person on earth is here in the plaza. Each of them has their own path for arriving there.

"That's why people talk with their angels. Because only the angels know the best path. It does no good to seek advice about it from others."

"Follow your dreams, and take your risks," they heard Valhalla saying.

"What will this world be like?"

"It will be only for those who enter into paradise," Paulo answered. "The world of the 'Conspiracy.' The world of people who are able to see the transformations that are occurring, of people who have the courage to pursue their dreams and listen to angels. A world for all those who believe in that world."

A murmur arose from the crowd, and Chris knew that the play had begun. She wanted to move forward to observe, but what Paulo was saying was more important.

"For centuries, we wept on the banks of the rivers of Babylon," Paulo continued. "We hung up our harps, we were prohibited from singing, we were persecuted and massacred. But we never forgot that there was a promised land. The Tradition survived everything.

"We learned how to fight, and we were strengthened by the battle. People are once again speaking of the spiritual world that only a few years ago was seen as something that only ignorant, complacent people believed in. There is an invisible thread that unites all those on the side of the light—like those joined kerchiefs of the Valkyries. And this thread is becoming a strong, shining rope, anchored by the angels. A handrail that is perceived by those who are most sensitive, and that will support us. Because we are many, and we are spread all over the earth. All of us moved by the same faith."

She said, "It's a world that has so many names, isn't it? New Age, Sixth Golden Age, Seventh Beam, and so on."

"But it's all the same world. I'll guarantee you."

Chris looked at Valhalla, there in the plaza, speaking of angels.

"Well, why is she trying to convince others?"

"No, no, she's not trying to convince them of anything. We all came from Paradise, we have spread throughout the world, and now we're returning there. Valhalla is asking these people to pay the price of that return."

Chris remembered the afternoon in the mine. "Sometimes it's a very high price."

"It may be. But there are people who are willing to pay it. They know that what Valhalla is saying is true, because it brings back something they had forgotten. All of them still carry in their soul memories and visions of Paradise. Years may go by without their remembering—until something happens: the birth of a child, a serious loss, a feeling of imminent danger, a sunset, a book, a song . . . or a group of women dressed in leather, speaking of God. Anything. Suddenly, these people remember.

"That's what Valhalla is doing. Reminding them that a place exists. Some of them are listening, others aren't—those who aren't will pass by the gates without seeing that they're open."

"But she's talking about this new world."

"Those are just the words she uses. Actually, they have retrieved their harps from the willows, and are playing them again—and millions of people all over the world are singing of the joys of the Promised Land. No one is alone anymore."

They heard the sound of motorcycles. The play was over. Paulo began to walk toward the car.

"Why didn't you ever tell me about all this?" she asked.

"Because you already knew."

Yes, she had known. But only now did she remember.

❖

The Valkyries rode from city to city on their motorcycles, with their trappings, their kerchiefs, and their strange outfits. And they spoke of God.

Paulo and Chris went with them. When they made camp on the outskirts of a city, the couple stayed in hotels. When they stopped in the middle of the desert, they slept in the car. They made a campfire, and the dangers of the desert receded— the animals did not approach. As they dropped off to sleep, they could look up at the stars and hear the howls of the coyotes in the distance.

Ever since the afternoon at the mine, Paulo had been practicing the channeling process. He was afraid that Chris might think that he hadn't really known what he had tried to teach her.

"I know J.," she said, when the subject came up. "You don't have to prove your knowledge to me."

"My girlfriend back in those days also knew the person who was teaching me," he answered.

They sat down together every afternoon, working at the destruction of their second minds; they prayed for their angels, and tried to invoke their presence.

"I believe in this new world," he said to Chris, when they had completed yet another exercise in channeling.

"I know you believe in it. Or you wouldn't have done the things you've done during your lifetime."

"But, even so, I don't know whether the things I do are really correct."

"Give yourself some credit," she answered. "You're doing the best you can—very few people would travel so far to find their angel. And don't forget, you broke the pact."

The pact he had broken in the mine: J. was going to be happy about that! Although Paulo was almost certain that he already knew everything, J. hadn't tried to argue Paulo out of this trip to the desert.

When the two had completed their channeling exercises, they talked for hours about angels. But only between themselves—Valhalla never again spoke of the matter.

ONE AFTERNOON, AFTER THEIR CONVERSA-
tion, he went to talk with Valhalla.

"You know the Tradition," he said. "You cannot
interrupt a process once you have begun it."

"I'm not interrupting anything," she answered.

"But soon I'll have to go back to Brazil. And I
haven't yet accepted forgiveness, nor made a bet."

"I'm not interrupting the process," she said
again.

She suggested that they take a walk out in the
desert. When they reached a certain point, they sat
down together and watched the sunset, and talked
about rituals and ceremonies. Valhalla asked about
J.'s teaching methods, and Paulo wanted to know
what the results were of her preaching in the
desert.

"I'm preparing the path," she said casually. "I
am doing my part, and I expect to do it right
through to the end. Then, I'll know what the next
step is."

"How are you going to know when the time
comes to stop?"

Valhalla pointed to the horizon. "We have to
make eleven trips through the desert, pass through
the same places eleven times and repeat the same
things eleven times. That's all I was told to do."

"Your master said that?"

"No, the archangel Michael."

"And what trip is this?"

"This is the tenth."

The Valkyrie put her head on Paulo's shoulder, and they sat in silence for a long time. He had a desire to caress her, put her head in his lap, as she had done for him at the abandoned mine. She was a warrior, but she, too, needed to rest.

He thought about it for some time, but decided against it. And the two returned to the camp.

As the days passed, Paulo began to suspect that Valhalla was teaching him everything he needed to know—but that, as Gene had done, she was doing it without directly showing him the path. He began to observe closely what the Valkyries did; he thought he might perceive some clue, some teaching, a new practice. And, when Valhalla called him to go with her at day's end—something she did every day now—he decided that he would discuss things with her.

"There's nothing that prevents you from teaching me directly," he said. "You are not a master. It's not like it is with Gene, or J., or even with me—people who know two Traditions."

"Yes, I am a master. I learned through revelation. You're right that I don't pronounce curses, and I don't participate in covens, nor am I a member of any secret societies. But I know many things that you don't know, because the archangel Michael taught them to me."

"Well, that's why I'm here. To learn."

The two were seated in the sand, leaning against some rocks.

"I need affection," she said. "I really need affection."

Paulo shifted his position, and Valhalla laid her head in his lap. They sat there for some time, looking out at the horizon.

It was Paulo who spoke first. He didn't want to raise the subject, but felt he had to.

"I'm going away soon, you know."

He awaited her reaction. She said nothing.

"I have to learn how to see my angel. I feel as if you have been trying to teach me, but that I'm not seeing it."

"No. My teachings are as clear as the desert sun."

Paulo caressed the hair that covered his lap.

"You have a beautiful wife," Valhalla said.

Paulo understood the comment, and took his hands away.

When he had rejoined Chris that night, he told her what Valhalla had said about her. Chris smiled, but said nothing.

THEY CONTINUED TO TRAVEL WITH THE
Valkyries. Even after Valhalla's comment—about
the clarity of her teachings—Paulo continued to
pay close attention to everything the Valkyries did.
But the routine varied little: travel along, speak in
public places, perform the rituals he already knew,
and move on.

And make love. They made love to men they
met along the way. Usually they were groups on
motorcycles, bold enough to approach the Valkyries.
When this happened, there was a tacit agreement
that Valhalla would have the right to first choice. If
she wasn't interested, any of the others could approach the newcomer.

The men never knew this. They were made to
feel that they were with the woman they had chosen—but the choice had been made much earlier.
By the women.

The Valkyries drank beer and talked of God.
They performed sacred rituals, and made love out
among the rocks. In the larger cities, they went to
some public place to perform their miracle play—
getting those who were in the audience to participate.

At the end, they asked for contributions.
Valhalla never played a role, but she directed every-

thing that was happening. Afterward, she would pass her kerchief around, and she always received money.

Every afternoon, before Valhalla called Paulo to walk with her in the desert, he and Chris practiced their channeling and talked with their angels. Although the channel was not yet completely opened, they felt the presence of constant protection, of love and peace. They heard phrases that made little sense, they had some intuitions, and many times the only sensation was one of joy—nothing more. But they knew they were speaking to their angels, and that the angels were happy at this.

Yes, the angels were happy, because they had been contacted again. Any person who resolved to speak with them would discover that it was not the first time. They had already conversed with them when they were children—the angels had appeared in the form of "secret friends," and had been their companions in long conversations and in play, protecting them from evil and from danger.

And every child had spoken with their guardian angel—until that day when their parents noticed that the child was talking to people who "didn't exist." Then they became intrigued, blamed it on excessive childish imagination, consulted with

educators and psychologists, and came to the con-
clusion that the child should give up that sort of behavior.

The parents always insisted on telling their children that their secret friends didn't exist—perhaps
because they had forgotten that they too had spoken to their angel at one time. Or, who knows, perhaps they thought they lived in a world where
there was no longer any place for angels. Disen-
chanted, the angels had returned to God's side,
knowing that they could no longer impose their
presence.

But a new world was beginning. The angels
knew where the gates to Paradise were, and they
would conduct all who believed in them to those
gates. Perhaps they needn't even believe—it was
enough that they *needed* angels, and the angels
would return gladly.

PAULO SPENT HIS NIGHTS TRYING TO understand why Valhalla was doing as she did—putting things off.

Chris knew the answer. And the Valkyries knew the answer, as well—even though none of them said anything about it.

Chris was waiting for the blow to fall. Sooner or later it was going to happen. That's why Valhalla had not left them, had not taught them what else they needed to know about meeting with their angel.

ONE AFTERNOON, IMMENSE MOUNTAIN formations began to appear off to the right side of the road as they drove. Soon, to the left, mountains and canyons could be seen, and a gigantic salt flat, gleaming in the sun, extended from one side to the other.

They had arrived at Death Valley.

The Valkyries made camp close to Furnace Creek—the only place for miles around where there was water. Chris and Paulo decided to stay with the group, because the only hotel for miles was filled.

That night, the entire group sat around the campfire, chatting about men and motorcycles, and—for the first time in many days—angels. As they always did before sleeping, the Valkyries knotted together their kerchiefs, held the long cord that was formed, and once again repeated the psalm that sang of the rivers of Babylon and of the harps hanging in the willow trees. They could never forget that they were warriors.

When the ritual was over, silence fell over the encampment, and everyone made their sleeping arrangements. Except Valhalla.

She walked some distance from the camp, and gazed for a long time at the moon. She asked the archangel Michael to continue to appear to her, to continue to provide her with valuable advice, and to help her to maintain a firm hand.

"You won in your battles with the other angels," she prayed. "Teach me to win. That I not disperse this flock of eight people, so that one day we might be thousands, millions. Forgive my errors, and fill my heart with enthusiasm. Grant me the strength to be both man and woman, both hard and soft.

"May my word be your lance.

"May my love be your scale."

She made the sign of the cross, and fell silent, listening to the howl of a coyote in the distance. She was wakeful, and began to think back on her life. She remembered when she had been just an employee at the Chase Manhattan Bank, and when her life amounted to nothing more than her husband and her two children.

"Then I saw my angel," she said to the silent desert. "The angel appeared to me, enveloped in light, and asked that I take on this mission. I was not forced, there were no threats, nor any promise of reward. My angel simply asked."

She had left the next day, and went straight to the Mojave Desert. She began preaching alone, speaking of the open gates to Paradise. Her husband divorced her and won custody of the children. She didn't really understand clearly why she had accepted this mission, but every time she wept out of pain and solitude, her angel told her stories of other women who had accepted messages from God: the Virgin Mary, Saint Theresa, and Joan of Arc. The angel said that all the world needed was an example. People who were capable of following their dreams and of fighting for their ideas.

She lived for almost a year outside Las Vegas. She exhausted the little money she had been able to pull together, went hungry, and slept outdoors. Until one day, a poem came into her hands.

The poem told the story of a saint, Maria Egipciaca. She was traveling to Jerusalem, and had no money to pay for her passage across a river. The boatman, eyeing the attractive woman, suggested to her that, although she had no money, she did have her body. Maria Egipciaca surrendered herself to the boatman. When she arrived at Jerusalem, an angel appeared and blessed her for what she had done. And, although today almost no one remembers her, she was canonized by the church following her death.

Valhalla interpreted the story as a sign. She preached in God's name during the day, and twice a week went to the casinos, became the lover of wealthy men, and was able to put together some money. She never asked her angel whether she was doing the right thing—and her angel said nothing.

Little by little, led by the invisible hands of other angels, her companions began to arrive.

"One more trip," she said again, aloud, to the silent desert. "Only one more trip to complete my mission, and then I can get back to the world. I have no idea what awaits me, but I want to get back. I need love, affection. I need someone who can protect me here on earth, just as my angel protects me in heaven. I have done my part; I have no regrets, even though it was awfully hard."

She made the sign of the cross again, and returned to the encampment.

SHE SAW THAT THE BRAZILIAN COUPLE was still seated by the campfire, gazing at the flames.

"How many days until your fortieth?" she asked Paulo.

"Eleven."

"Well then, tomorrow night, at ten o'clock, in Golden Canyon, I will make you accept forgiveness. The Ritual That Demolishes Rituals."

Paulo was astonished. She was right! The answer had been under his nose the whole time!

"Using what?" he asked.

"Using hatred," Valhalla answered.

"That's fine," he said, trying to conceal his surprise. But Valhalla knew that Paulo had never used hatred in the Ritual That Demolishes Rituals.

She left the couple and went to where Rotha, the youngest of the Valkyries, was sleeping. She affectionately caressed the girl's face to awaken her—Rotha might have been making contact with the angels that appear in one's sleep, and Valhalla didn't want to interrupt the conversation. Rotha finally opened her eyes.

"Tomorrow night, you are going to learn how to accept forgiveness," Valhalla said. "And then you will be able to see your angel."

"But I'm already a Valkyrie."

"Of course. And even if you are not able to see your angel, you will still be a Valkyrie."

Rotha smiled. She was twenty-three, and was proud to be roaming the desert with Valhalla.

"Don't wear your leather outfit tomorrow. Not from the moment the sun rises until the end of the Ritual That Demolishes Rituals."

She embraced her with great affection. "Go back to sleep," she said.

※

Paulo and Chris continued to sit by the fire for another half hour. Then they arranged some of their clothing as pillows, and prepared to sleep. They had thought about purchasing sleeping bags at every large city they had passed through, but they couldn't bring themselves to shop around. More than anything, they always hoped to find a hotel somewhere. So, when it was necessary to camp out with the Valkyries, they either had to sleep in the car or near the fire. Their hair had already been scorched several times by blowing sparks—but nothing any more serious had happened until now.

"What did she mean?" Chris asked as they lay there.

"Nothing important." He had had a couple of beers, and was sleepy.

But Chris pressed the matter. She wanted an answer.

"Everything in life is a ritual," Paulo said. "For witches as much as for those who have never heard of witchcraft. Both are always trying to perform their rituals to perfection."

Chris knew that those on the magical path had their rituals. And she understood, as well, that there were rituals in everyday life—marriages, baptisms, graduations.

"No, no. I'm not talking about those obvious rituals," he went on impatiently. He wanted to sleep, but she pretended not to have sensed his irritation. "I'm saying that everything is a ritual. Just as a mass is a great ritual, composed of various parts, the everyday experience of any person is, also.

"A carefully elaborate ritual that the person tries to perform precisely, because he or she is afraid that—if any part is left out—everything will go wrong. The name of that ritual is *Routine*."

He decided to sit up. He was groggy because of the beers he had drunk, and if he continued to lie down, he would be unable to complete his explanation.

"When we are young, we don't take anything too seriously. But slowly, this set of daily rituals becomes solidified, and takes us over. Once things have begun to go along pretty much as we imagined they would, we don't dare risk altering the ritual. We like to complain, but we are reassured by the fact that each day is more or less like every other. At least there is no unexpected danger.

"That way, we are able to avoid any inner or outer growth, except for the kinds that are provided for within the ritual: so many children, such and such a kind of promotion, this and that kind of financial success. When the ritual becomes consolidated, the person becomes a slave."

"Does that happen sometimes with those on the path?"

"Of course. They use the ritual to make contact with the invisible world, to destroy the second mind, and to enter into the Extraordinary. But, for us too, the terrain we conquer becomes familiar. And we feel the need to seek out new territories. But any magus is fearful of changing the ritual. It's a fear of the unknown, or a fear that other rituals won't function as well—but it is an irrational fear, a strong one, that never disappears without some help."

"And what is the Ritual That Demolishes Rituals?"

"Since a magus is unable to change their rituals, the Tradition decides to change the magus. It's a kind of Sacred Theater in which the magus has to play a different character."

He lay down again, turned on his side, and pretended to sleep. Chris might ask for further explanations. She might want to know why Valhalla had mentioned hatred.

Negative emotions were never invoked in the sacred theater. On the contrary, people who participated in that kind of theater tried to work with the good, and to assume characters that were strong, enlightened. That way, they were able to convince themselves that they were better people than they had thought, and—when they believed that—their lives changed.

To work with negative emotions would mean the same thing. He would wind up convincing himself that he was worse than he had imagined.

THEY SPENT THE AFTERNOON OF THE following day exploring Golden Canyon, a series of ravines with tortuous curves and walls about twenty feet high. At the moment that the sun set, while they were doing their channeling exercise, they saw how the place had acquired its name: The brilliant minerals embedded in the rock reflected the rays of the sun, causing the walls to appear to be carved out of gold.

"Tonight there will be a full moon," Paulo said.

They had already seen the full desert moon, and it was an extraordinary spectacle.

"I awoke today thinking about a passage in the Bible," he continued. "It's from Solomon: 'It is good that you retain this, and that you not take away your hand from it; for whoever fears the Lord will emerge from everything unscathed.'"

"A strange message," Chris said.

"Very strange."

"My angel is speaking to me more and more," she told him. "I'm beginning to understand the words. I understand perfectly well what you were talking about in the mine, because I never believed that this communication with my angel could happen."

That made Paulo feel pleased. And together they contemplated afternoon's end. This time, Valhalla had not appeared for their walk in the desert.

The glistening stones they had seen that afternoon were no longer apparent. The moon cast a strange, phantasmagorical light into the ravine. They could hear their own footsteps in the sand, as they walked along in silence, alert to any sound they might hear. They didn't know where the Valkyries were meeting.

They came almost to the end point, where the fissure widened to form a small clearing. No sign of them.

Chris broke the silence. "Maybe they decided against it."

She knew that Valhalla was going to prolong the game as long as possible. But Chris wanted it to be over.

"The animals are on the prowl. I'm afraid of the snakes," she said. "Let's go back."

But Paulo was looking upward.

"Look," he said. "They haven't decided against it."

Chris followed his gaze. At the top of the rocks that formed the right wall of the ravine, the figure of a woman was looking down at them.

She felt a shiver.

The figure of another woman appeared. And another. Chris went to the middle of the clearing; she could see three more women on the other side.

Two were missing.

"WELCOME TO THE THEATER!" VALHALLA'S voice echoed from the stone walls. "The audience is already here, and they await the spectacle!"

That was how Valhalla had always begun her plays in the city parks.

But I'm not part of the spectacle, Chris thought. *Maybe I should climb up there with them.*

"Here, the price of admission is paid upon leaving," the voice continued, repeating what was always said in the city squares. "It may be a high price, or we might return what is paid. Do you want to take the risk?"

"Yes, I do," Paulo answered.

"What is all this?" Chris suddenly shouted. "Why such dramatics, why so much ritual, why all of this just to see an angel? Isn't it enough to speak with the angel? Why don't you do as everyone else does: simplify the way we make contact with God and with what is sacred in this world?"

There was no response. Paulo felt that Chris was ruining everything.

"The Ritual That Demolishes Rituals," said one of the Valkyries from high in the rocks.

"Silence!" Valhalla shouted. "The audience gets to speak only when this is over! Applaud or boo—but pay the admission!"

Valhalla finally appeared. She wore her kerchief knotted around her forehead, Indian-style. She usually wore it that way when she was saying her prayers at day's end. It was her crown.

She brought with her a barefoot girl, wearing Bermudas and blouse. When they had come closer, and the moonlight illuminated their faces, Chris saw that it was one of the Valkyries—the youngest of the group. Without her leather outfit and her aggressive air, she seemed only a child.

Valhalla placed her in front of Paulo, and traced a large square around them. At each of its corners, she stopped and spoke a few words. Paulo and Rotha repeated the words in Latin—the young woman made several errors, and had to begin again.

She doesn't even know what she's saying, Chris thought. Neither the square nor the words were a part of what usually happened at the performances in the city.

When Valhalla had completed the inscription of the square, she asked that the two approach her. They remained within the square, while she stood outside.

Valhalla turned to Paulo, looked deep into his eyes, and handed him the long leather belt she usually wore around her waist.

"Warrior, you are imprisoned within your destiny by the power of these lines and of these sacred names. Warrior, victorious in battle, you are now in your castle, and you will receive your reward."

In his mind, Paulo created the walls of the castle. From that moment on, the ravine, the Valkyries, Chris, Valhalla, and everything else ceased to be of importance.

He was an actor in the sacred theater. The Ritual That Demolishes Rituals.

"Prisoner," Valhalla said to the girl, "your defeat has been humiliating. You were unable to defend your army with honor. The Valkyries will come down from heaven to recover your body when you are dead. But until then, you will receive the punishment that the loser deserves."

With an abrupt gesture, she tore open the girl's blouse.

"Let the spectacle begin! This, oh warrior, is your trophy!"

He seized the girl violently. She fell awkwardly, cutting her chin, and it bled.

Paulo knelt at her side. In his hand, he clutched Valhalla's belt, and it seemed to have an energy of its own. It frightened him, and for a few moments he left the imaginary walls of the castle and returned to the ravine.

"She's really hurt," Paulo said. "She needs some help."

"Warrior, that is your trophy!" Valhalla repeated, stepping away. "The woman who knows the secret you are after. Extract that secret from her, or give it up forever."

"Not for ourselves, Lord, not for ourselves, but for the glory of your name," he said in a low voice, repeating the motto of the Templars. He had to make a quick decision. He recalled the time when he believed in nothing, thinking all of this was simply dramatics—but even then, things were transformed, and the truth emerged.

He was faced with the Ritual That Demolishes Rituals. A sacred moment in the life of a magus.

"Sed nomini Tuo de Gloriam," he said again. And in the moment that followed, he dressed himself in the role suggested by Valhalla. The Ritual That Demolishes Rituals began to unfold. Nothing else was important—only that unknown path, that frightened woman at his feet, and a secret that had to be won from her. He strode around his victim, and thought of those times when morality

was different—when taking possession of a woman was a rule of combat. Men had risked their lives in war for gold and women.

"I won!" he screamed at the girl. "And you lost!"

He knelt and seized her by the hair. Her eyes stared into his.

"It is we who will win," the girl said.

He threw her violently to the ground again.

"The rule of victory is to win."

"All of you think you won," the prisoner continued. "You won only a battle. It is we who will win the war."

Who was this woman who dared to speak to him this way? She had a lovely body—but that could wait. He had to learn the secret he had sought for so long.

"Teach me how to see my angel," he said, trying to keep his voice calm. "Then you will be set free."

"I am free."

"No. You don't know the rules of victory," he said. "That's why we defeated all of you."

The woman seemed to become confused. "Tell me about those rules," she said. "And I will tell you the secret about your angel."

The prisoner was making a trade. He could torture her, destroy her. There she was, fallen at his feet—yet she was proposing a trade. Perhaps she wouldn't confess under torture. Better to make the trade. He would tell her about the five rules of victory, since she was never going to leave there alive.

"The morality rule: You have to fight on the side that is in the right, and that's why we won. The weather rule: A war in the rain is different from a war in the sun; a battle in the winter is different from a battle in the summer."

He could fool her now. But he wasn't able to invent false rules on the spot. The woman would notice his hesitancy.

"The space rule," he continued. "A war in a ravine is different from a war in the field. The choice rule: The warrior knows how to choose who should give advice, and who will remain at his side in combat. A chieftain cannot be surrounded by cowards or traitors."

He thought for a moment about whether he should continue. But he had already told her four of the rules.

"The strategy rule." he said finally. "The way in which the battle is planned."

That was all of it. The girl's eyes gleamed.

"Now tell me about the angels."

She looked at him, saying nothing. She had learned the formula, even though it was too late. Those valiant warriors never lost a battle—and legend had it that they used five rules of victory. Now she knew what they were.

She knew it would do her no good, but at least she could die in peace. She deserved the punishment she was to receive.

"Tell me about the angels," the warrior said again.

"No! I won't tell you about the angels."

The warrior's eyes changed, and she was delighted. He would show no mercy. The only thing that frightened her was that the warrior might be governed by the rule of morality, and spare her life. She wasn't deserving of that. She was guilty—dozens, hundreds of sins accumulated during her short life. She had disappointed her parents, disappointed men who had grown close to her. Deceived the warriors who had fought at her side. She had allowed herself to be taken prisoner—she was weak. She deserved to be punished.

"Hatred!" they heard a distant woman's voice say. "The secret of the ritual is hatred!"

"We made a trade," the warrior repeated, and

now his voice was as cold as steel. "I lived up to my side."

"You are not going to let me leave alive," she said. "But at least I got what I wanted. Even though it's of no use to me."

"Hatred!" The voice of the woman was beginning to have an effect on him. He was allowing his worst feelings to surface. Hatred was permeating the warrior's heart.

"You are going to suffer," he said. "The worst tortures anyone has ever experienced."

"I will suffer."

"I deserve this," she thought. She deserved the pain and the punishment. She deserved death. Ever since she was a child, she had refused to fight—she didn't believe that she was capable of it. She accepted everything from others, suffered in silence the injustices to which she fell victim. She wanted everyone to see that she was a good girl. That she was sensitive in her heart, and able to help everyone. She wanted to be liked at any cost. God had given her a good life, and she had not been able to make use of it. Instead, she begged that others love her, lived her life as others wanted her to, all in order to show that she was kindhearted and able to please everyone.

She had been unfair to God, had thrown her life away. Now she needed an executioner who would dispatch her quickly to hell.

The warrior felt the belt becoming alive in his hand. For a moment, his eyes met those of his prisoner.

He was waiting for her to change her mind, beg his forgiveness. Instead, the prisoner winced as she awaited the blow.

Suddenly, everything disappeared except his rage at having been tricked by his prisoner. The hatred came in waves, and he was beginning to see how capable he was of cruelty. He had always been wrong, he had always allowed his heart to give in at the very moment when he should have meted out justice. He had always forgiven—not because he was a good person, but because he was a coward. He was afraid that he couldn't see such things through to the end.

Valhalla looked at Chris, and Chris returned her stare. The moonlight prevented each from seeing clearly into the eyes of the other. And that was a good thing, because each was afraid to reveal what she was feeling.

"For God's sake!" the prisoner screamed again, before the blow was delivered.

The warrior halted his stroke in midair.

But the enemy had arrived.

"Enough," said Valhalla. "That's enough."

Paulo's eyes were glazed. He grabbed Valhalla by the shoulders.

"I feel this hatred!" he shouted. "I'm not making it up! I've let some demons loose that I wasn't even aware of!"

Valhalla took the belt from his hand, and went to see whether Rotha was injured.

She was crying, her head between her knees.

"It was all true," she said, embracing Valhalla. "I provoked him, and I used him as my instrument of punishment. I wanted him to destroy me, to put me to death. My parents blamed me, my brothers and sisters blamed me. All I've ever done in life was wrong."

"Go and put on another blouse," said Valhalla.

Rotha stood up, trying to arrange her torn clothing.

"I want to stay this way," she said.

Valhalla hesitated for a moment, but said nothing. She walked to the wall of the canyon and began to climb. At the top, she was surrounded by three Valkyries, and she gave a signal that the others climb up, as well.

Chris, Rotha, and Paulo climbed the wall in silence. The moonlight showed them the way; with the many handholds in the rocks, it was not a difficult ascent. At the top, they could look out at a vast plain riven by arroyos.

Valhalla told Paulo and the girl to come together again, face to face, embracing.

"Did I hurt you?" Paulo asked. He was horrified with himself.

Rotha shook her head. She was ashamed—she would never succeed at becoming a woman like those who surrounded her. She was too weak.

Valhalla knotted together the kerchiefs of two of the Valkyries. She slipped them through the belt loops of the man and woman, binding them to each other. From where she stood, Chris could see that the moon formed a halo around the couple. It would have been a beautiful scene—if it were not for all that had happened. If that man and woman were not so distant from each other—or so close.

"I am unworthy of seeing my angel," Rotha said to Valhalla. "I am weak, and my heart is filled with shame."

"I am unworthy of seeing my angel," Paulo said, so that all could hear. "I have hatred in my heart."

"I have loved many," Rotha said. "But spurned true love."

"I have nourished hatred for years, and avenged myself over things that were unimportant," Paulo continued. "I was always forgiven by my friends, but never learned how to forgive them in return."

Valhalla turned to face the moon.

"We are here, archangel. The Lord's will be done. Our inheritance is hatred and fear, humiliation and shame. The Lord's will be done.

"Why was it not enough simply to close the gates to Paradise? Did you also have to cause us to carry hell in our hearts? But, if that is the will of the Lord, you must know that all of humanity has been doing his will for generations and generations."

Then Valhalla began to stride in circles around the couple, chanting.

"THIS IS THE PREFACE, THE SALUTATION.

"Praised be Our Lord Jesus Christ, forever may he be praised.

"Guilty warriors are speaking to You.

"Those who have always used the best weapons they have—against themselves.

"Those who deem themselves unworthy of blessings. Those who believe that happiness is not for them. Those who suffer more greatly than others do.

"Those who arrived at the gates of freedom, gazed at paradise, and said to themselves: 'We should not enter. We are not deserving.' They are speaking to You.

"Those who one day experienced the judgment of others, and concluded that most of them were right. They are speaking to You.

"Those who judge and condemn themselves. They are speaking to You."

ONE OF THE VALKYRIES HANDED THE BELT
to Valhalla, and she raised it toward heaven

●

"This is the first element: Air.

"Here is the belt. If we are that way, punish us.

"Punish us because we are different. Because we have dared to dream, and to believe in those things no one else any longer believes in.

"Punish us because we challenged what exists, what everyone else accepts, what most others want to remain unchanged.

"Punish us because we speak of faith, and we feel hopeless. We speak of love, but we receive neither the affection nor the comfort we feel we deserve. We speak of freedom, and we are prisoners to our own guilt.

"Lord, even were I to raise this belt high, high enough to touch the stars, I would not touch your hand.

"Because your hand covers our heads. And it caresses us, and you say to us: 'Suffer no more. I have already suffered enough.'

"You say to us: 'Like you, I dreamed, and I believed in a new world. I spoke of love, and at the same time, asked our Father to end my ordeal. I challenged what was. What the majority cared not to change. I thought I was wrong when I performed my first miracle: changing water to wine, simply to enliven a party. I felt the hard stare of others, and I shouted, "Father, Father, why have you forsaken me?"'

"They have already used the belt on me. You need suffer no more."

VALHALLA THREW THE BELT TO THE ground, and scattered sand to the wind.

●

"This is the second element: Earth.

"We are a part of this world, Lord. And this world is filled with our fears.

"We will write our sins in the sand, and it will be the desert wind's task to scatter them.

"Keep our hands strong, keep us from ceasing to struggle, even though we judge ourselves unworthy of going into battle.

"Make use of our lives, nourish our dreams. If we are made of the Earth, the Earth is also made of us. Everything is only one thing.

"Teach us and use us. We are forever yours.

"The Law was reduced to one commandment: 'Love your neighbor as yourself.'

"If we love, the world changes. The light of love scatters the darkness of guilt.

"Keep us strong in love. Make us accept for ourselves the love of God.

"Show us our love for ourselves.

"Require us to seek out the love of others. Even with fear of rejection, of severe glances, of the

hardness of heart of some—do not permit us ever
to give up our quest for love."

ONE OF THE VALKYRIES HELD OUT A TORCH
to Valhalla. She lit it, and held up the blazing torch
to heaven

◉

"This is the third element: Fire.

"You say, Lord: 'I came to set fire to the Earth.
And I am watchful that the fire grow.'

"May the fire of love grow in our hearts.

"May the fire of transformation glow in our
movements.

"May the fire of purification burn away our
sins.

"May the fire of justice guide our steps.

"May the fire of wisdom illuminate our path.

"May the fire that spreads over the Earth never
be extinguished. It has returned, and we carry it
within us.

"Prior generations passed on their sins to suc-
ceeding ones. Thus has it been, down to our fa-
thers.

"Now, though, we will pass forward the torch
of your fire.

"We are warriors of the light, this light that we
carry with pride.

"The fire that, when kindled for the first time, showed us our faults and our sins. We were surprised and frightened, and we felt ourselves to be incapable.

"But it was the fire of love. And it consumed what was bad in us when we accepted it.

"It showed us that we are neither better nor worse than those who frowned at us.

"And for this we accept forgiveness. There is no more guilt, and we can return to paradise. And we will bring with us the fire that will burn on earth."

Valhalla inserted the torch into a crevice in the rocks. Then she opened her canteen and spilled a few drops of water on Paulo's and Rotha's heads.

"This is the fourth element: Water.

"You said: 'Whoever drinks of this water will never thirst.'

"Well then, we are drinking this water. We wash away our sins, for love of the transformation that is going to shake the Earth.

"We will hear what the angels say, we will be messengers of their words.

"We will do battle with the best weapons and the speediest of horses.

"The gates are open. We are worthy to enter."

"LORD JESUS CHRIST, WHO SAID TO HIS apostles, 'My peace I leave you, my peace I give you,' do not look at our sins, but at the faith that animates your assembly."

Chris knew that passage. It was similar to one used in the Catholic service.

"Lamb of God, who takes away the sins of the world, have pity on us," Valhalla concluded, untying the kerchiefs that joined Paulo and Rotha.

"You are free."

Then Valhalla approached Paulo.

The sting, thought Chris. *Now comes the serpent's sting. It's the payment. She's in love. If the Valkyrie tells him what the price is, he will pay with pleasure. And I won't be able to say a thing—because I'm just an ordinary woman, and I know nothing about the laws in the world of angels. None of them knows that I have already died many times here in the desert, and been reborn so many times, as well. They don't know that I have been speaking to my angel, and that my soul has grown. They're used to me, and they know how I think. I love him. She is only enamored.*

❁

"Now, it's you and me, Valkyrie! The Ritual That Demolishes Rituals!"

Chris's scream echoed out over the sinister desert, bathed in the light of the moon.

Valhalla was expecting the scream. She had already dealt with guilt, and knew that what she wanted was no crime. Only a caprice. She was entitled to cultivate her caprices—her angel had taught her that such things took no one away from God, or from the sacred task each person had to perform in their life.

She remembered the first time she had seen Chris, at the luncheonette. A shiver had coursed through her body, and strange intuitions—intuitions she was unable to understand—had taken hold of her. *The same thing must have happened to her,* she thought.

Paulo? She had completed her mission with him. And, although he didn't know it, the price she had charged was high—as they had traveled through the desert, she had learned many rituals that J. used only with his disciples. He had told her everything.

She also desired him as a man. Not for what he was, but for what he knew. A caprice, and her angel forgave capriciousness.

She looked again at Chris, and thought, *This is my tenth round. I too need to change. This woman is an instrument of the angels.*

Never taking her eyes from Chris, the Valkyrie said, "The Ritual That Demolishes Rituals. May God tell us what our characters should be!"

She had accepted the challenge. Her moment for growth had arrived.

The two women began to walk around the circumference of an imaginary circle, like cowboys of the old West before a gunfight. Not a sound could be heard—it was as if time had stopped.

The other Valkyries understood what was happening because they were all women, accustomed to fighting for love. And they would do so through to the ultimate consequences, using every trick and artifice. They would do so for love, the justification for their lives and their dreams.

Chris's character began to emerge. She donned the leather outfit, and tied the kerchief around her head. Between her breasts shone the medallion of the archangel Michael. She had dressed herself as a strong character, as the woman she admired and would like to be: She was Valhalla.

Chris gestured with her head, and the two stood still. Valhalla felt as though she were standing before a mirror.

Looking at Chris, she could see herself. She knew the arts of war by heart, but had forgotten the lessons of love. She knew the five rules of victory, and had slept with every man she desired, but she had forgotten the art of love.

She regarded herself as reflected by this other person; she had enough power to defeat her. But her own character was emerging, taking form, and this character, although it was also possessed of sufficient power, was not used to this type of battle.

She had transformed herself into a woman in love, who marched with her man, carrying his sword when necessary, and protecting him from all danger. She was a strong woman, although she appeared to be a weak one. She was a person who walked the path of love, regarding it as the only possible road to wisdom. A path where mysteries were revealed through surrender and forgiveness. She was seeing it with such clarity!

Valhalla had assumed the character of Chris.

And Chris saw herself, reflected in the other.

Chris began to walk slowly toward the precipice. Valhalla did the same, and both approached the abyss. A fall from there would be fatal. But they were women who would recognize no limits. Chris stopped at the very edge, allowing time for Valhalla to do so, as well.

The floor of the desert was thirty feet below, and the moon was thousands of miles above. Between the moon and the desert floor, two women confronted each other.

"He is my man. Don't covet him merely out of capriciousness. You don't love him," Chris said.

Valhalla didn't respond.

"I'm going to take one more step," Chris continued. "I'll survive. I'm a courageous woman."

"I'll do it with you," answered Valhalla.

"Don't. You know about love now. It's a huge world, and you will have to spend the rest of your life trying to understand it."

"I will step back if you will. You know about your strength now. Your horizon now extends to mountains, valleys, and deserts. Your soul has grown large, and will continue to grow. You've discovered your courage, and that's enough."

"Enough, if what I taught you is sufficient to pay the price you were going to charge me."

A long silence. Then the Valkyrie walked over to Chris.

And kissed her.

"I accept that as the price," she said. "Thank you for what you have taught me."

Chris removed the watch from her wrist. It was all she had to offer.

"Thank you for what you taught me, too," she said. "Now I know about my strength. I would never have learned about it, though, unless I had come to know a strange, beautiful, powerful woman."

With great tenderness, she placed the watch on Valhalla's wrist.

THE SUN SHONE DOWN ON DEATH VALLEY. The Valkyries tied their kerchiefs around their faces, leaving only their eyes exposed.

Valhalla approached the couple. "You cannot go with us. You have to talk to your angel."

"There's one thing left," Paulo said. "The bet."

"Bets and pacts are made with the angels. Or with the devils."

"I still don't know how to see my angel," he answered.

"You have already broken a pact. You have already accepted forgiveness. The bet you must make with your angel."

The other women's motorcycles roared. She placed the kerchief across her face, mounted her bike, and turned to Chris.

"I will always be a part of you," Chris said. "And you will always be a part of me."

Valhalla removed a glove and threw it to Chris. Then she revved her engine and the cycles sped away, leaving behind a gigantic cloud of dust.

A MAN AND A WOMAN WERE TRAVELING across the desert. On some days, they stopped at cities with thousands of inhabitants, and on others, in towns with just one motel, a restaurant, and a gas station. They kept to themselves—and each afternoon they walked out through the rocks and the sand, feeling as if they had returned to the place where the first star was about to be born. And there, they talked with their angels.

They heard voices, gave advice to one another, and remembered things that seemed to have been completely forgotten sometime in the past.

She had completed her communication with the protection and wisdom of her angel, and was now gazing at the desert sunset.

He sat there, waiting. He wanted his angel to descend and appear in blazing glory. He had done everything right, and now he had simply to wait.

He waited one, two, three hours. He rose only when night had completely fallen; he found his wife, and they returned to the city.

They had dinner, and returned to the hotel. She went to bed and pretended to sleep, while he stared into space.

She got out of bed in the middle of the night, and went to where he sat, asking him to come to bed. She said that she was afraid of sleeping alone because of a bad dream. He lay down beside her, quietly.

"You are already communicating with your angel," he had grown used to saying at such times. "I've heard you speaking when you are channeling. You say things you would never say in ordinary life. Wise things. Your angel is here."

He caressed her, but continued to lie there in silence. She asked herself if his sadness was really because of the angel, or perhaps had to do with some lost love.

This question remained locked inside.

Paulo was thinking about the woman who had left, but that wasn't what made him disconsolate. Time was passing, and soon he would have to return to his own country. He would meet again with the man who had taught him that angels exist.

That man, Paulo imagined, *will tell me that I did enough. That I broke a pact that needed to be broken, that I accepted forgiveness that I should have accepted long ago. Yes, that man will continue to teach me about the path to wisdom and love, and I will get closer and closer to my angel. I'll speak with my angel every day, giving thanks for protection and asking for help. And that man will tell me that it is sufficient.*

Yes, because J. had taught him from the beginning that there are frontiers. That it was necessary
to go as far as possible—but that there were certain
times when one had to accept the mystery, and understand that each person had his own gift. Some
knew how to cure, others possessed words of wisdom, while others conversed with spirits. It was
through the sum of such gifts that God could
demonstrate his glory, using humankind as his instrument. The gates to paradise would be open to
those who had resolved that they would pass
through them. The world was in the hands of those
who had the courage to dream—and to realize
their dreams.

Each to their own talent. Each to their own gift.

But none of that consoled Paulo. He knew that
Gene had seen his angel. That Valhalla had seen her
angel. That many others had written books and
stories and reports telling of their meetings with
their angels.

And he had not been able to see his own.

197

IN SIX MORE DAYS, THEY WOULD HAVE TO leave the desert. They stopped in a small city called Ajo, where most of the inhabitants were elderly. It was a place that had known its moments of glory—when the mine there had brought jobs, prosperity, and hope to the inhabitants. But, for some reason—unknown to any of them—the company had sold its houses to the employees and closed the mine.

Paulo and Chris sat in a restaurant, drinking coffee and waiting for the cool evening to arrive. An old woman asked if she could sit with them.

"All of our children have gone away," she told them. "No one is left except the old-timers. Some day, the entire city will disappear, and all our work, everything we built, will no longer mean a thing."

It had been a long time since anyone had even passed through the place. The old woman was happy to have someone to talk to.

"People come here, build, and hope that what they are doing is important," she continued. "But overnight, they find that they are demanding more of the Earth than it has to give. So, they abandon everything and move on, without thinking about the fact that they have involved others in their dream—others who, weaker than they, have to stay behind. Like with the ghost towns out there in the desert."

Maybe that's what's happening to me, Paulo thought. *I brought myself here, and I've abandoned myself.*

He recalled that once an animal trainer had told him how he was able to keep his elephants under control. The animals, as infants, were bound by chains to a log. They would try to escape, but could not. They tried throughout their entire infancy, but the log was stronger than they were.

So they became accustomed to captivity. And when they were huge and strong, all the trainer had to do was place the chain around one of their legs and anchor it anywhere—even to a twig—and they would not attempt to escape. They were prisoners of their past.

The long hours of daylight seemed to have no end. The sky caught fire, the Earth baked, and they had to wait, wait, wait—until the color of the desert changed again to softer tones of pink. That was when he could leave the city, try his channeling, and once again await the appearance of his angel.

"Someone once said that the earth produces enough to satisfy needs, but not enough to satisfy greed," the old woman continued.

"Do you believe in angels?" Paulo asked her.

The woman was astonished at the question. But that was all that Paulo wanted to talk about.

"When you're old, and death isn't too far off, you begin to believe in anything," she said. "But I don't know if I believe in angels."

"They exist."

"Have you ever seen one?" There was a mixture of incredulity and hope in her eyes.

"I talk with my guardian angel."

"Does your angel have wings?"

It was the question everyone asked. Yet he had forgotten to ask it of Valhalla.

"I don't know. I haven't seen my angel yet."

The woman considered whether she should get up and leave. The solitude of the desert made some people strange. But maybe this man was joking with her, just passing the time.

She wanted to ask where the couple came from, and what they were doing in a place like Ajo. She hadn't been able to identify their strange accent.

Maybe they're from Mexico, she thought. But they didn't look like Mexicans. She would ask when the opportunity arose.

"I don't know if you two are fooling around with me," she said, "but, as I said, I'm getting close to death. I suppose I could last another five or ten years. Maybe even twenty. But at my age, you certainly realize you're going to die."

"I know that I'm going to die, too," Chris said.

"No, not like an old person does. For you, it's a remote idea. It might happen some day. For us, it's something that could happen tomorrow. That's why many elderly people spend the time remaining to them looking only in one direction: the past. It's not that they're so fond of their memories, but they know that looking in that direction they won't see anything to be feared.

"Very few old people look to the future, and I'm one of them. When we look into the future, we see what it holds for us: death."

Paulo didn't say anything. You can't say anything new about awareness of death to those who practice magic, but he knew the woman would leave the table if she knew that he was a magus.

"That's why I'd like to believe that you both are serious. That angels really exist."

"Death is an angel," Paulo said. "I have seen it twice in this incarnation, but very briefly. There wasn't enough time to see its face. But I know people who have seen, and I know others that were oppressed by Death, and later told me about it.

They said that Death has a handsome face, and a gentle touch."

The old woman stared at Paulo. She wanted to believe him.

"Does Death have wings?"

"This angel is made of light," he answered. "When the moment comes, Death assumes the form that is easiest for you to deal with."

The old woman thought about that. Then she stood up.

"I'm not afraid anymore. I have prayed, and asked that the angel of death have wings when it comes to me. My heart tells me that my wish will be granted."

She kissed them both. It was no longer important to her where they came from.

"It was my angel that sent you both. Thank you so much."

Paulo remembered Gene. He too had been an angel's instrument. Thinking of Gene, Paulo realized that he and Chris had also served as the instruments of an angel.

AT SUNSET, THEY WENT TO A MOUNTAIN not far from Ajo. They sat facing the east, waiting for the first star to appear. When that occurred, they would initiate their channeling activity.

They called this process Contemplation of the Angel. It was the first ceremony they had created after the Ritual That Demolishes Rituals had swept the others away.

"I never asked," Chris said as they waited. "Why it is that you want to see your angel?"

"Well, you've already explained to me a number of times that it didn't matter at all to you."

His voice had a sarcastic tone. She pretended not to notice.

"Okay. But it's important for you. Can you tell me why?"

"I've already explained that. The day of our meeting with Valhalla."

"You don't need a miracle," she insisted. "You're just being capricious."

"There's nothing capricious in the spiritual world. Either you accept it, or you don't."

"So? Haven't you accepted this, your world? Or was everything you said a lie?"

She must be thinking of that story in the mine, Paulo thought. It was a difficult question to answer, but he was bound to try.

"I've already witnessed a number of miracles," he began. "Many miracles. You and I have even witnessed some together. We watched J. create openings in the clouds, fill the darkness with light, move objects from one place to another.

"You've seen me read people's minds, cause the wind to blow, perform rituals involving power. I've seen magic function many times in my life—both for evil and for good. I have no doubts about it."

He paused. "But we have also become used to miracles. And we always want to see others. Faith is a difficult conquest, and it requires daily combat in order to be maintained."

It was time for the star to appear, and he had to end his explanation. But Chris interrupted.

"It's been that way with our marriage, too," she said. "And I'm exhausted."

"I don't understand. I'm speaking about the spiritual world."

"The only reason I'm able to understand what you're saying is because I know your love," she said. "We've been together for a long time. But after the first two years of joy and passion, every day

began to be a challenge for me. It's been very difficult to keep the flames of our love alive."

She regretted having brought up the subject—
but now she was going to see it through.

"Once you told me that the world was divided
into the farmers, who love the Earth and the har-
vest, and the hunters, who love the dark forests and
conquest. You said I was a farmer, like J. That I
walked the path of wisdom, achieved through contemplation. And you said I was married to a
hunter."

Her thoughts were pushing their way out, and
she couldn't stop herself. She was afraid the star
might appear before she had finished.

"And I am married to a hunter. I know that, and
its been very difficult being married to you! You're
like Valhalla, like the Valkyries. They never rest.
They deal only in the strong emotions of the hunt,
of taking risks. Of the darkness of night and the
taking of prisoners. At the beginning, I didn't think
I'd be able to live with that. I, who was looking for
a life like everybody else's, married to a magus! A
magus whose world is governed by laws I don't
even know—a person who feels he is alive only
when he is facing challenges."

She looked into his eyes.

"Isn't J. a much more powerful magus than you are?"

"Much wiser," Paulo answered. "Much more experienced. He follows the path of the farmer, and it is on that path that he finds his power. I'll be able to achieve my power only by following the path of the hunter."

"Well then, why did he accept you as a disciple?"

Paulo laughed. "For the same reason that you chose me as a husband. Because we're different from one another."

"Valhalla, you, and all your friends think only in terms of the Conspiracy. Nothing else is important—you're all fixated on this business of changes, of a new world to come. I believe in that new world, too—but, God, does it have to be this way?"

"What way?"

She thought for a minute. She didn't know exactly what he was getting at. "This way that always involves conspiracies."

"That's *your* word for it."

"But I know it's true. And you confirmed it."

"I said that the gates of paradise are open, for a certain time, to all who desire to enter. But I also said that each person has his or her own path—and only one's angel can say which is the correct one."

Why am I acting this way? What's going on with me? she thought. She remembered the engravings she had seen as a child, of angels leading children to the edge of an abyss. She was surprised at what she had been saying here. She had fought many times with him, but she had never spoken about magic in the way that she was now.

Yet her soul had grown during these forty days in the desert, she had learned about her second mind, she had crossed swords with a powerful woman. She had died many times, and was stronger each time she was reborn.

The hunt actually gave me great pleasure, she thought.

Yes. That's what was driving her crazy. Because, since the day she had challenged Valhalla to the duel, she had had the feeling that she had wasted her entire previous life.

No, she thought. *I can't accept that. I know J. He is a farmer-type, and an enlightened person. I spoke with my angel before Paulo did. I know how to speak to my angel as well as Valhalla does—even though the language is still a bit strange.*

But she was apprehensive. Perhaps she had been wrong in choosing how she wanted to live her life. *I've got to keep talking,* she thought. *I have to convince myself that I didn't make the wrong choice.*

"You need yet another miracle," she said. "And you will always need yet another. You will never be satisfied, and you will never understand that the kingdom of heaven cannot be conquered by force."

God, make his angel appear, because it's so important to him! Make me be wrong, Lord.

"You're not even giving me a chance to talk," he said.

But at that moment, the first star appeared on the horizon.

It was time for channeling.

THEY SAT DOWN, AND, AFTER A BRIEF period of relaxing, began to concentrate on the second mind. Chris couldn't stop thinking about Paulo's last comment—she really hadn't permitted him to talk.

Now it was too late. She had to allow her second mind to recite its boring problems. To voice the same concerns, over and over. Her second mind that night wanted to get at her heart. It was saying she had chosen the wrong path, and had found her true destiny only when she had experimented with the Valhalla character.

It was telling her that it was too late to change, that her life had been a failure, that she would spend the rest of her life following her husband—without experiencing the pleasures of the dark forest and the taking of prisoners.

It was telling her she had chosen the wrong husband—that she would have been better off marrying a farmer-type. It was telling her that Paulo had other women, and that those women were hunter-types that he met on the night of the full moon, and at secret magic rituals. It was telling her that she should leave him, so that he could be happy with a woman who was his equal.

She argued several times—saying that it wasn't important that she knew there were other women, that she wouldn't leave him on that account. Because love isn't logical or rational. But her second mind came back at her—so she decided not to argue. She would just listen quietly until the conversation went silent and died out.

Then a kind of fog began to envelop her thinking. The channeling had begun. An indescribable sensation of peace took hold of her, as if the wings of her angel were covering the entire desert, preventing anything bad from happening. Whenever she did her channeling, she felt a great love for herself and for the universe.

She kept her eyes open, so as not to lose her awareness, but the cathedrals began to appear. They emerged, enveloped in mist, immense churches she had never visited, but that existed somewhere in the world. During her early days of channeling, she'd had only confused impressions, indigenous songs blending with meaningless words; but now her angel was showing her cathedrals. That seemed to make some sort of sense, although she couldn't quite understand it.

In the beginning, they had only been trying to begin a conversation. With each day that passed, she was able to understand her angel better. Soon, there would be a level of communication as clear as the one she enjoyed with anyone who spoke her own language. It was only a matter of time.

THE ALARM ON PAULO'S WATCH SOUNDED. Twenty minutes had passed. The channeling was over.

She looked at him, knowing what was going to happen now. He would sit there without saying a word, sad and disappointed. His angel hadn't appeared. They would return to the small motel in Ajo, and he would take a walk while she tried to sleep.

She waited until he stood, and then stood up, as well. But there was a strange gleam in his eye.

"I will see my angel," he said. "I know I will. I made the bet."

"The bet, you will have to make with your angel," Valhalla had said. She had never said, "The bet, you will have to make with your angel, *when he appears.*" Yet, that's what Paulo had understood her to mean. He had waited for an entire week for his angel to appear. He was ready to make any bet, because the angel was the light, and the light was what justified human existence. He trusted in that light, in the same way that, fourteen years earlier, he had doubted the darkness. In contrast with the traitorous experience with the darkness, the light established its rules beforehand—so that whoever accepted them was knowingly committing to love and compassion.

He had already met two of the three conditions, and almost failed with regard to the third—the simplest of them! But his angel's protection had prevailed, and, during the channeling ... ah, how good it was to have learned to converse with the angels! Now he knew that he would be able to see his angel, because he had met the third condition.

"I broke a pact. I accepted forgiveness. And, today, I made a bet. I have faith, and I believe," he said. "I believe that Valhalla knows the method for seeing one's angel."

Paulo's eyes were shining. There would be no nocturnal walks, no insomnia tonight. He was absolutely certain that he was going to see his angel. Half an hour ago, he had asked for a miracle—but that was no longer important.

So that night it would be Chris's turn to be sleepless, and to walk the deserted streets of Ajo, imploring God to make a miracle, because the man she loved needed to see his angel. Her heart was squeezed more tightly than ever. Perhaps she preferred a Paulo who was in doubt. A Paulo who needed a miracle. A Paulo who appeared to have lost his faith. If his angel appeared, fine; if not, he could always blame Valhalla for having erred in her teaching. That way, he would not have to learn the most bitter lesson that God taught, when he closed the gates to paradise: the lesson of disappointment.

But instead, here was a man who seemed to have bet his life against the certainty that angels could be seen. And his only guarantee was the word of a woman who rode the desert, speaking of new worlds to come.

Perhaps Valhalla had never even seen an angel. Or maybe what worked for her didn't work for others—hadn't Paulo said that? Maybe he hadn't heeded his own words.

Chris's heart grew smaller and smaller as she saw the light in Paulo's eyes.

And at that moment, his entire face began to glow.

"Light!" he screamed. "Light!"

She turned. On the horizon, near where the first star had appeared, three lights shone in the sky.

"Light!" he said again. "The angel!"

Chris had a strong desire to kneel down and give thanks, because her prayer had been answered, and God had sent his army of angels.

Paulo's eyes filled with tears. The miracle had happened. He had made the right bet.

They heard a roar to their left, and another over

their heads. Now there were five, six lights gleaming in the sky; the desert was alight.

For a moment she lost her voice. She, too, was seeing his angel! The bursts of sound were becoming stronger and stronger, passing to the left, passing to the right, over their heads, wild thunderbursts that didn't come from the sky, but from behind, from the side—and moved toward where the lights were.

The Valkyries! The true Valkyries, daughters of Wotan, galloping across the sky, carrying their warriors! She blocked her ears in fear.

She saw that Paulo was doing the same—but his eyes appeared to have lost their brilliance.

Immense balls of fire grew on the desert horizon, and they felt the ground shake under their feet. Thunder in the sky and on the Earth.

"Let's go," she said.

"There's no danger," he answered. "They're military planes. Far from here."

But the supersonic fighters broke the sound barrier close to where they stood, with a terrifying sound.

The two clung to each other as they watched the spectacle with fascination and terror. Now there were balls of fire on the horizon, and green lights. There were more than a dozen, falling slowly from the sky, illuminating the entire desert so that no one and nothing could remain hidden.

"It's just a military exercise," he reassured her. "The Air Force. There are a lot of bases around here. I've seen them on the map." Paulo had to shout to make himself heard. "But I wanted to believe they were angels."

They're the instruments of angels, she thought. *Angels of death.*

The yellow brilliance of the bombs falling on the horizon blended with the bright green lights falling slowly by parachute. Everything below was visible, and the planes were unerring as they dropped their mortal loads.

The exercise lasted for half an hour. And, just as suddenly as they had arrived, the planes disappeared, and silence returned to the desert. The last of the green lights came to earth and died. The ground no longer trembled, and they could see the stars again.

Paulo took a deep breath. He closed his eyes, and concentrated: *I won the bet. I'm absolutely sure I won the bet.* His second mind was coming and going, saying no, that it was all in his imagination, that his angel would not show himself. But he dug the nail of his index finger into his thumb until the pain was insupportable; pain always banishes nonsensical thinking.

"I will see my angel," he repeated, as they descended the mountain.

Her heart squeezed again. But she didn't want to allow him to see how she felt. The only way to change the subject quickly was to listen to what her second mind was saying, and to ask Paulo if it made sense.

"I want to ask you something," she said.

"Don't ask·me about the miracle. It will happen or it won't. Let's not waste our energy discussing it."

"No, it's not about that."

She hesitated. Paulo was her husband. He knew her better than anyone did. She was fearful of his response, because what he said carried more weight than what others said. But she resolved that she would ask the question anyway; she couldn't stand keeping it inside.

"Do you think I chose wrong?" she asked. "That I've wasted my life sowing seeds, content to watch the crops flourish around me instead of experiencing the strong emotions of the hunt?"

He walked along, looking up at the sky. He was still thinking about his bet, and about the planes.

"Often I look at people like J.," he said. "People like J., who are at peace, and through that peace, find communion with God. I look at you, able to talk with your angel before I was—even though it was I who came here to do that. I watch you sleeping so soundly, while I'm standing at the window, and I ask myself why the miracle I'm waiting so desperately for doesn't happen. And I ask myself: Did I choose the wrong path?"

He turned to her. "What do you think? Did I choose the wrong path?"

Chris took his hand in hers. "No. You would be very unhappy."

"And so would you if you had chosen mine."

"That's a good thing to remember."

BEFORE THE ALARM WENT OFF, HE SAT UP in bed without making a sound.

He looked outside, and it was still dark.

Chris was asleep. For a moment, he thought of waking her, and telling her where he was going. That she should say a prayer for him. But he decided against it. He could tell her everything when he returned. It wasn't as if he were heading for any place dangerous.

He switched on the light in the bathroom, and filled his canteen from the faucet. Then he drank as much water as he could swallow—he had no idea how long he would be out there.

He dressed, grabbed the map, and memorized his route. Then, he got ready to leave.

But he couldn't locate the key to the car. He looked in his pockets, in his knapsack, on the bedside table. He considered lighting the lamp—but no, it might awaken her, and the light from the bathroom was enough. He couldn't spend any more time looking—every minute spent here was a minute less that he could devote to waiting for his angel. Within four hours, the heat of the desert would be unbearable.

Chris hid the key, he thought. She was a different woman now—she was speaking to her angel, and her intuition had increased considerably. Perhaps she had guessed at what his plans were and was frightened.

Why would she be frightened? That night when he has seen her at the precipice with Valhalla, he and Chris had made a sacred agreement; they had promised that never again would they risk their lives in the desert. Several times, the angel of Death had passed close to them, and it wouldn't be smart to keep testing the patience of their guardian angel. Chris knew him well enough to know that he would never fail to keep a promise. That's why he was stealing away before the first rays of the sun were to be seen—to avoid the dangers of the night, and the dangers of the day.

Nevertheless, she was concerned, and had hidden the key.

He went to the bed, having decided to awaken her. And he stopped.

Yes, there was a reason. She wasn't worried about his safety, or about the risks he might take. She was fearful, but it was a different kind of fear— that her husband might be defeated. She knew that Paulo would try something. Only two days remained before they left the desert.

It was a good idea to do what you did, Chris, he

thought, laughing to himself. *A defeat such as this would take two years to overcome, and for the whole time you would have to put up with me, spend sleepless nights with me, bear with my bad moods, suffer my frustration along with me. It would be much worse than these days I lived through, before I learned how to make my bet.*

He looked through her things; the key was in the security belt where she kept her passport and her money. Then he remembered his promise about safety—all this may have been a reminder. He had learned that you never go out into the desert without leaving at least some indication of your destination. Even though he knew that he would be back soon, and even knowing that his destination, after all, was not that far away—and that if anything were to happen, he could even return on foot—he decided not to run the risk. After all, he had promised.

He placed the map on the bathroom sink. And he used the can of pressurized shaving foam to make a circle around a location: Glorieta Canyon.

Using the same means, he sprayed a message on the mirror:

I WON'T MAKE ANY MISTAKES.

Then he put on his sneakers, and left.

When he was about to put the key into the ignition, he found he had left his own key there.

She must have had a copy made, he thought. *What did she think was going to happen? That I was going to abandon her in the middle of the desert?*

Then he recalled Gene's strange behavior when he had forgotten the flashlight in the car. Thanks to the matter of the key, Paulo had marked the place where he was heading. His angel was seeing to it that he took all the necessary precautions.

❖

The streets of Borrego Springs were deserted. *Just like in the daytime,* he thought to himself. He remembered their first night there, when they had stretched out on the floor of the desert, trying to imagine what their angels would be like. Back then, all he wanted to do was talk to his.

He turned to the left, out of the city, and headed for Glorieta Canyon. The mountains were to his right—the mountains they had descended by car back when they had first arrived. *Back then,* he thought, and realized it hadn't been all that long ago. Only thirty-eight days.

But, as with Chris, his soul had died many times

out there in the desert. He was pursuing a secret that he already knew, and had seen the sun turn into the eyes of death. He had met up with women who appeared to be angels and devils at the same time. He had reentered a darkness he thought he had forgotten. And he had discovered that, although he had spoken so often of Jesus, he had never completely accepted the Savior's forgiveness.

He had reencountered his wife—at the very moment when he believed he had lost her forever. Because (and Chris could never know it) he had fallen in love with Valhalla.

That was when he had learned the difference between infatuation and love. Like conversing with the angels, it was really very simple.

Valhalla was a fantasy. The warrior woman, the huntress. The woman who conversed with angels, and was ready to run any risk in order to surpass her limits. For her, Paulo was the man who wore the ring of the Tradition of the Moon, the magus who knew about the occult mysteries. The adventurer, capable of leaving everything behind to go out in search of angels. Each would always be fascinated by the other—so long as each remained exactly what the other imagined.

That's what infatuation is: the creation of an image of someone, without advising that someone as to what the image is.

But some day, when familiarity revealed the true identity of both, they would discover that behind the Magus and the Valkyrie there was a man and a woman. Each possessing powers, perhaps, each with some precious knowledge, maybe, but— they couldn't ignore the fact—each basically a man and a woman. Each with the agony and the ecstasy, the strength and the weakness of every other human being.

And when either of them demonstrated how they really were, the other would want to flee—because it would mean the end of the world they had created.

He found love on a cliff where two women had tried to stare each other down, with the full moon as a backdrop. And love meant dividing the world with someone. He knew one of the women well, and had shared his universe with her. They had seen the same mountains, and the same trees, although each had seen them differently. She knew his weaknesses, his moments of hatred, of despair. Yet she was there at his side.

They shared the same universe. And although often he had had the feeling that their universe contained no more secrets, he had discovered—that night in Death Valley—that the feeling was wrong.

He stopped the car. Ahead, a ravine pierced the mountain. He had chosen the place based on its name—actually, angels are present at all times and in all places. He got out, drank some more of the water that now he always carried in bottles in the trunk of the car, and fixed the canteen to his belt.

He was still thinking about Chris and Valhalla as he made his way to the ravine. *I think I'll probably be infatuated many more times,* he said to himself. He felt no guilt about it. Infatuation was a good thing. It gave spice to life, and added to its enjoyment.

But it was different from love. Love was worth everything, and couldn't be exchanged for anything.

He stopped at the mouth of the ravine and looked out over the valley. The horizon was shading to crimson. It was the first time he had seen the dawn out in the desert; even when they had slept out in the open, the sun was always up when he awoke.

What a beautiful sight I've been missing, he thought. The peaks of the mountains in the distance were gleaming, and pink streaks were creeping into the valley, coloring the stones and the plants that survived there virtually without water. He gazed at the scene for some time.

He was thinking of a book he had written, in which—at a certain point—the shepherd, Santiago, climbs to the top of a mountain to look out over the desert. Except for the fact that Paulo was not atop a mountain, he was surprised at the similarity to what he had written about eight months earlier. He had also just realized the significance of the name of the city where he had disembarked in the United States.

Los Angeles. In Spanish: The Angels.

But this wasn't the time to be thinking of the signs he had seen along the way.

"This is your face, my guardian angel," he said aloud. "I see you. You have always been there before me, and never have I recognized you. I hear your voice. Every day I hear it more clearly. I know you exist, because they speak of you in all corners of the earth.

"Perhaps one man, or even an entire society, can be wrong. But all societies and all civilizations, everywhere on the planet, have always spoken of angels. Nowadays, children and the elderly and the prophets are listening. They will continue to speak of angels down through the centuries, because prophets, children, and old people will always exist."

A blue butterfly fluttered about him. It was his angel, responding.

"I broke a pact. I accepted forgiveness."

The butterfly drifted from one side to the other. He had seen numbers of white butterflies in the desert—but this one was blue. His angel was content.

"And I made a bet. That night, up on the mountain, I bet all of my faith in God, in life, in my work, in J. I bet everything I had. I bet that, when I opened my eyes, you would show yourself to me. I placed my entire life on one tray of the scales. I asked that you place your countenance on the other.

"And, when I opened my eyes, the desert was before me. For a few moments, I thought I had lost. But then—ah, how lovely the memory is—then, you spoke."

A streak of light appeared on the horizon. The sun was coming alive.

"Do you remember what you said? You said: 'Look around, this is my face. I am the place where you are. My mantle will cover you with the rays of the sun in daytime, and with the glow of the stars at night.' I heard your voice clearly!

"And then you said: 'Always need me.'"

His heart was content. He would wait for the sun to rise, and look for a long time at the face of his angel. Later, he would tell Chris of his bet. And tell her that seeing one's angel was even easier than speaking with him! One had only to believe than angels exist, only to need the angels. And they would show themselves, as brilliant as the rays of morning. And they would help, performing their task of protection and guidance, so that each generation would speak to the next of their presence—so that they would never be forgotten.

Write something, he heard a voice within him say.

Strange. He wasn't even trying to do his channeling. All he wanted to do was see his angel.

But some being within him was demanding that he write something. He tried to concentrate on the horizon and the desert, but that's all he could manage.

He went to the car and picked up a pen and some paper. He had had some experience with automatic writing, but had never gone deeply into it—J. had said that it wasn't for him. That he should seek out his true gift.

He sat down on the floor of the desert, pen in hand, and tried to relax. Before long, the pen would begin to move itself, would produce some strokes, and then words would follow. In order for this to happen, he had to lose a bit of his awareness, and allow something—a spirit or an angel—to take him over.

He surrendered completely, and accepted his role as instrument. But nothing happened. *Write something,* he heard the voice within him say again.

He was fearful. He wasn't going to be incorporated by some spirit. He was channeling, without meaning to—as if his angel were there, speaking to him. It wasn't automatic writing.

He took a different grip on the pen—now with firmness. The words began to emerge. And he wrote them down, without time even to think of what he was writing:

For Zion's sake, I will not hold my peace.
And for Jerusalem's sake, I will not rest,
Until her righteousness goes forth as
    brightness,
And her salvation, as a lamp that burns.

This had never happened before. He was *hearing* a voice within him, dictating the words:

You shall be called by a new name,
Which the mouth of the Lord will name.
You shall also be a crown of glory in the hand
    of the Lord,
And a royal diadem in the hand of your God.
You shall no longer be termed Forsaken,
Nor your land anymore be termed Desolate;
But you shall be called Hephzibah,
For the Lord delights in you, and your land
    shall be married.

He tried to converse with the voice. He asked to whom he should say this.

It has already been said, the voice answered. *It is simply being remembered.*

Paulo felt a lump in his throat. It was a miracle, and he gave thanks to God.

The golden globe of the sun was rising above the horizon. He put down the pad and pen, stood up, and held out his hands in the direction of the light. He asked that all of that energy of hope—hope that a new day brings to millions of people on the face of the earth—would enter through his fingers and repose in his heart. He asked that he might always believe in the new world, in the angels, and in the open gates to paradise. He asked for protection by his angel and the Virgin Mary—for him, for all whom he loved, and for his work.

The butterfly came to him and, responding to a secret sign from his angel, landed on his left hand. He kept absolutely still, because he was in the presence of another miracle: His angel had responded.

He felt the universe stop at that moment: the sun, the butterfly, and the desert there before him.

And in the next moment, the air around him trembled. It wasn't the wind. It was a shock of air—the same as one feels when a car is passed by a bus at high speed.

A shiver of absolute terror ran up his spine.

SOMEONE WAS THERE.

"Do not turn around," he heard the voice say.

His heart was pounding, and he was beginning to feel dizzy. He knew it was fear. A terrible fear. He remained motionless, his arms extended before him, the butterfly poised on his hand.

I'm going to pass out, he thought.

"Do not pass out," the voice said.

He was trying to maintain control of himself, but his hands were cold, and he began to tremble. The butterfly flew away, and he lowered his arms.

"Kneel down," the voice said.

He knelt. He couldn't think. There was nowhere to go.

"Clear the ground,"

He did as the voice ordered. With his hands, he brushed a small area in the sand directly in front of him so that it was smooth. His heart continued to beat rapidly, and he was feeling more and more dizzy. He thought he might even have a heart attack.

"Look at the ground."

An intense light, almost as strong as the morning sun, shone on his left side. He didn't want to look directly at it, and wished only that everything would end quickly. For a moment, he recalled his childhood, when appearances of Our Lady had been described to children. He had passed many sleepless nights as a child, asking God never to order the Virgin to appear to him—because the prospect was so frightening. Scary.

The same fright that he was experiencing now.

"Look at the ground," the voice insisted.

He looked down at the area he had just swept clear. And that was when the golden arm, as brilliant as the sun, appeared, and began to write in the sand.

"This is my name," the voice said.

The fearful dizziness continued. His heart was beating even faster.

"Believe," he heard the voice say. "The gates are open for a while."

He gathered every bit of strength he had remaining.

"I want to say something," he said aloud. The heat of the sun seemed to be restoring his strength.

He heard nothing. No answer.

❁

An hour later, when Chris arrived—she had awakened the hotel owner, and demanded that he drive her there—he was still looking at the name in the sand.

THE TWO OTHERS WATCHED AS PAULO prepared the cement.

"What a waste of water, out in the middle of the desert," Gene joked.

Chris asked him not to kid around, since her husband was still feeling the impact of his vision.

"I found where the passage came from," Gene said. "It's from Isaiah."

"Why that passage?" Chris asked.

"I have no idea. But I'm going to remember it."

"It speaks about a new world," she continued.

"Maybe that's why," Gene answered. "Maybe that's why."

Paulo called to them.

The three said a Hail Mary. Then Paulo climbed to the top of a boulder, spread the cement, and placed within it the image of Our Lady that he always carried with him.

"There. It's done."

"Maybe the guards will take it away when they find it here," Gene said. "They watch over the desert as if it were a flower garden."

"Maybe," Paulo said. "But the spot will still be marked. It will always be one of my sacred places."

"No," Gene said. "Sacred places are individual places. In this one, a text was dictated. A text that already existed. One that speaks of hope, and had already been forgotten."

Paulo didn't want to think about that now. He was still fearful.

"In this place, the energy of the soul of the world was felt," Gene said. "And it will be felt here forever. It is a place of power."

They gathered up the plastic sheeting in which Paulo had mixed the cement, placed it in the trunk of the car, and left to take Gene back to his old trailer.

"Paulo!" he said when they were saying their good-byes. "I think it would be good for you to know an old saying from the Tradition: *When God wants to drive a person insane, he grants that person's every wish.*"

"Could be," Paulo answered. "But it was worth it."

EPILOGUE

One afternoon, a year and a half after the angel's appearance, a letter arrived for me in Rio, from Los Angeles. It was from one of my Brazilian readers living in the United States, Rita de Freitas, and was in praise of *The Alchemist*.

On impulse, I wrote to her, asking that she go to a canyon near Borrego Springs to see whether the statue of Our Lady of Aparecida was still there.

After I had mailed the letter, I thought to myself: *That's pretty silly. This woman doesn't even know me. She's just a reader who wanted to say a few kind words, and she'll never do as I've asked. She's not going to get into her car, drive six hours into the desert, and see whether a small statue is still there.*

Just before Christmas in 1989, I received a letter from Rita, from which I have excerpted the following:

There have been some marvelous "coincidences." I had a week off from my job over the Thanksgiving holiday. My boyfriend (Andrea, an Italian musician) and I were planning on getting away to someplace different.

Then your letter arrived. And the place you mentioned was near an Indian reservation. We decided to go . . .

... On our third day there, we went to look for the canyon, and found it. It was on Thanksgiving Day. It was interesting, because we were driving very slowly, but saw no sign of the statue. We came to the end of a canyon, stopped, and began climbing to the top of the cliff there. All we saw were the footprints of coyotes.

At this point, we concluded that the statue couldn't any longer be there ...

As we were returning to the car, we saw some flowers among the rocks. We stopped the car and got out. We saw some small candles burning, some golden cloth with a butterfly woven into it, and a straw basket that had been thrown aside. We decided that must have been the place where the statue had been placed, but it was no longer there.

What was interesting was the fact that I'm sure none of that was there when we had first passed by. We took a photograph—enclosed—and went on our way.

When we were almost at the mouth of the canyon, we saw a woman dressed in white. Her clothing seemed Arabian—turban, long tunic—and she was walking in the middle of the road. Very strange—how could a woman such as this appear out of nowhere, in the middle of the desert?

I was thinking: Could this be the woman who had placed those flowers and lighted the candles? There was no car to be seen, and I wondered how she could have come there.

But I was so surprised that I couldn't bring myself to talk to her.

I examined the photo Rita had sent: It was exactly where I had placed the statue.

It was Thanksgiving Day. And I'm certain that angels were there that day.

I wrote this book in January/February 1992, shortly after the end of the Third World War—where the battles were much more sophisticated than those fought with conventional arms. According to the Tradition, this war began in the 1950s, with the blockade of Berlin, and ended when the Berlin Wall fell. The victors divided up the defeated empire, as in a conventional war. The only thing that didn't occur was a nuclear holocaust—and this will never happen, because God's Work is too great to be destroyed by human beings.

Now, according to the Tradition, a new war will begin. An even more sophisticated war, survived by no one—because it is through its battles that man's growth will be completed. We will see the two armies—on one side, those who still believe in the human race, and know that our next step involves the growth of individual gifts. On the other side will be those who deny the future. Those who believe that life has a material ending, and—unfortunately—those who, although they have faith, believe that they discovered the path to enlightenment, and want the others to follow it with them.

That's why the angels have returned and must be attended. Only they can show us the way—no one else. We can share our experiences—as I have tried to share mine in this book—but there is no formula for this growth. God has generously made His wisdom and His love available to us, and it is easy, very easy, to find them. One has only to understand channeling—a process so simple that it was difficult for me to recognize and accept. Since the combat will take place for the most part in the astral plane, it will be our guardian angels who will wield the swords and shields, protecting us from danger, and guiding us to victory. But our responsibility is huge, as well: We, at this moment in history, must develop our own powers. We must believe that the universe doesn't end at the walls of our room. We must accept the signs, and follow our heart and our dreams.

We are responsible for everything that happens in this world. We are the warriors of the light. With the strength of our love and of our will, we can change our destiny, as well as the destiny of many others.

The day will come when the problem of hunger can be solved through the miracle of the multiplication of the bread. The day will come when love will be accepted by every heart, and the most terrible of human experiences—solitude, which is worse than hunger—will be banned from the face of the Earth. The day will come when those who knock at the gates will see them open; those who ask will receive; those who weep will be consoled.

For the planet Earth, that day is still a long way off. But for each of us, that day can be tomorrow. One has only to accept a simple fact: Love—of God and of others—shows us the way. Our defects, our dangerous depths, our suppressed hatreds, our moments of weakness and desperation—all are unimportant. If what we want to do is heal ourselves first, so that *then* we can go in search of our dreams, we will never reach paradise. If, on the other hand, we accept all that is wrong about us—and despite it, believe that we are deserving of a happy life— then we will have thrown open an immense window that will allow Love to enter. Little by little, our defects will disappear, because one who is happy can look at the world only with love—the force that regenerates everything that exists in the Universe.

In *The Brothers Karamazov,* Dostoyevsky tells us the story of the Grand Inquisitor, which I paraphrase here:

During the religious persecutions in Sevilla, when all who did not agree with the Church were thrown into prison, or burned at the stake, Christ returns to earth and mixes in with the multitudes. But the Grand Inquisitor notes his presence, and orders him jailed.

That night, he goes to visit Jesus in his cell. And he asks why Jesus has decided to return at that particular moment. "You are making things difficult for us," the Grand Inquisitor says. "After all, your ideals were lovely, but it is we who are capable of putting them into practice." He argues that, although the Inquisition might be judged in the future to have been severe, it is necessary, and that he is simply doing his job. There is no use talking of peace when man's heart is always at war; nor speaking of a better world when there is so much hatred in man's heart. There was no use in Jesus' having sacrificed himself in the name of the human race, when human beings still feel guilty. "You said that all people are equal, that each has the divine light within, but you forgot that people are insecure, and they need someone to guide them. Don't make our work more difficult than it is. Go away," says the Grand Inquisitor, having laid out all of his brilliant arguments.

When he is finished, there is silence in the cell. Then Jesus comes to the Grand Inquisitor, and kisses him on the cheek.

"You may be right," Jesus says. "But my love is stronger."

❁

We are not alone. The world is changing, and we are a part of the transformation. The angels guide us and protect us. Despite all the injustice in the world, and despite the things that happen to us that we feel we don't deserve, and despite the fact that we sometimes feel incapable of changing what is wrong with people and with the world, and despite all of the Grand Inquisitor's arguments—love is even stronger, and it will help us to grow. Only then will we be able to understand the stars and miracles.

AUTHOR'S NOTE

Anyone who has read *The Valkyries* will know that this book is very different from *The Pilgrimage* (previously published as *The Diary of a Magus*), *The Alchemist,* and *Brida*.

It was an extremely difficult book to write. First, because it deals with matters that require sensitivity on the part of the reader. Second, because I have already told this story to many people, and I feared that I might have exhausted my capacity to write it down. This fear remained with me from the first page to the last, but—thank God—it was only a fear.

The third and most important reason: In order to relate the events that took place, I had to reveal details from my personal life—my marriage, my relationships with others, and the fragile distance that separates the magical Tradition to which I belong from the person I am. As is true for any human being, exposing my weaknesses and my private life is not easy.

But—as was made quite clear in *The Pilgrimage*—the path to magic is the path of the common people. One can have a master, follow the esoteric

Tradition, and possess the discipline needed to perform rituals; but the spiritual search is made up of many beginnings (thus the searcher is called an "initiate," someone who is always in the act of beginning something), and the only thing that matters—always—is the will to go on.

The Valkyries clearly presents the man that exists behind the magus, and this may disappoint those who are looking for "perfect beings," with their perfect truths regarding everything. But true seekers know that, regardless of our faults and defects, the spiritual path is stronger. God is love, generosity, and forgiveness; if we believe in this, we will never allow our weaknesses to paralyze us.

The events narrated in this book took place between September 5 and October 17, 1988. The sequential order of some of the events has been changed, and in two places I made use of fiction, only so that the reader could better grasp the matter at hand. But all of the essential events are true. The letter quoted in the Epilogue is on file at the Registry of Titles and Documents in Rio de Janeiro under number 478038.

Paulo Coelho